The Much-Adored Sandy Shore

The Much-Adored Sandy Shore

Angela Elwell Hunt

Tyndale House Publishers, Inc.
Wheaton, Illinois

For Gay and Dana

© 1992 Angela Elwell Hunt
Front cover illustration © 1992 by Ron Mazellan

Library of Congress Cataloging-in-Publication Data

Hunt, Angela Elwell, date
    The much-adored Sandy Shore / Angela Elwell Hunt.
        p.   cm. — (Cassie Perkins ; #5)
    Summary: To prove to her mother and stepfather that she is not
self-centered, Cassie decides to help an overweight high-school
classmate change her image.
    ISBN 0-8423-1065-7
    [1. Stepfamilies—Fiction. 2. Weight control—Fiction.
3. Alcoholism—Fiction. 4. High schools—Fiction. 5. Schools—
Fiction. 6. Conduct of life—Fiction.] I. Title. II. Series:
Hunt, Angela Elwell, date   Cassie Perkins ; #5.
PZ7.H9115Mu 1992
[Fic]—dc20   91-33411

Printed in the United States of America
99 98 97 96 95 94 93 92
8   7   6   5   4   3   2   1

Important People in My Life, by Cassie Perkins

1. Glen Perkins, my dad. ♥♥♥♥♥
   A systems analyst at Kennedy Space Center, and
   my favorite singer. Handsome, even if balding.
   Now divorced from my Mom and living in a
   condo. Sometimes I wonder if he gets lonely, but
   his work seems to keep him busy.

2. Claire Louise Perkins Harris, my mom. ♥♥♥♥♥
   An interior decorator. Now married to Tom Harris, a
   lawyer. Still has stars in her eyes, but only when her
   eyes are open. Baby Stephanie makes her tired a lot.

3. Stephanie Arien Harris, my new baby sister. ♥♥♥♥♥
   Or half sister. Whatever. The latest addition to our
   family, baby Steffie looks like me and screams like
   the devil.

4. Max Brian Perkins, my brother. ♥♥♥♥♥!
   Max lives with Dad in the condo. Max is the only
   ten-year-old in the tenth grade at my school. He's
   a genius, and he has epilepsy, which scares me to
   death, but Max deals with it. He says a lot of
   geniuses have had epilepsy.

5. Dribbles, my Chinese Pug. ♥♥♥♥
   She's just a puppy. Tom got her for me the day my
   old dog, Suki, died. I love her, but honestly, she

can be a pain. She's eaten two pairs of my shoes and my favorite purse.

6. Chip McKinnon, the guy I like. ♥♥♥♥
Chip's cute, funny, and best of all, dependable.

7. Tom Harris, my new stepfather. I hated him at first, but a lot has happened since then. At least I don't think he'll leave us, now that Stephanie's been born.

8. Nick Harris, my new stepbrother. Nick's in eleventh grade at a fancy prep school, and I think he's spoiled—a lot! I can't believe I ever thought he was *cute!*

9. Jacob A. Benton, or Uncle Jacob. ♥♥♥
He still won't tell me what the *A* stands for. He lives with us, and he's gruff and tough and runs the house. I really like him.

I couldn't help noticing Sandy Shore on Valentine's Day. I've known her for years as the *fat* girl in our class who's always kept to herself, but I'd never really thought about her. She's never done anything unusual, probably because being Sandy Shore is unusual enough.

But on Valentine's Day, Eric Brandt and some of his friends thought it'd be funny to send Sandy Shore flowers. The junior class was selling carnations for two dollars each to raise money for their prom. I guess Eric must have convinced a lot of his goony friends to shell out two bucks. Anyway, there in sixth period sat Sandy Shore at her desk in the corner of the room, with an armful of carnations.

The bright color of the flowers caught my eye. My face would have been red from embarrassment, but Sandy wasn't blushing at all. The carnations were blindingly red, and everyone saw them. If that had happened to me, I would have thrown the flowers in the garbage and run to the bathroom and cried for two hours. It was so obvious that the flowers were a joke because everyone knows Sandy is such a mess no one could possibly *like* her. She's overweight, and she's—well, she's not pretty. She never washes her hair, she just pulls it back into a dark, greasy pony-tail. Every single day she wears these homemade-looking tent dresses. In the winter, she wears a sweater *under* the tent. She also wears loafers with white ankle socks. Always white.

So there she was, Sandy Shore, sitting in class with her red carnations. As quiet as always. And she was smiling. It was a little gentle smile, but it was like she didn't even realize those flowers were supposed to be a dirty, rotten trick.

Eric Brandt and his friends sat on the other side of the room. They had laughed like crazy when Sandy came in with all those flowers, but when she didn't get upset or say anything, they just sat at their desks with their usual goony grins on their faces. They didn't know what to make of Sandy's smile. Jason Schmidt, a short kid who gets more than his share of trouble from Eric and his grunts, even turned around and whispered, "Say, Eric! Your girlfriend likes the flowers you sent her! Should I tell her you arranged the whole thing?"

Eric glared and clenched his fist in response, and

Jason turned back around. But he was still grinning, so I figured Eric's joke backfired.

Chip McKinnon, my boyfriend, thought of something else. "Hey, Eric," he whispered so Sandy wouldn't hear. "Sandy Shore's brother, Michael, is in the eleventh grade. What if he comes after you?"

Eric scowled at Chip, but then he slouched down in his chair and looked a little worried. He probably hadn't thought about Sandy's brother, and I couldn't help smiling. Michael Shore had a reputation as a troublemaker, and it would serve Eric Brandt right if Michael cornered him about sending Sandy flowers.

I looked over again at Sandy Shore, and I don't think she was even aware of what was going on. She just kept looking down at those flowers and smiling. How strange.

School wasn't the only place where strange things were happening. When I got home, Max was there. That's not the strange part—because it was Friday afternoon and Max comes to our house every other Friday afternoon and stays until Sunday night. That's the custody arrangement Mom and Dad made when they divorced two years ago.

The strange part was that Tom was in the library with his arm around Max, and they were getting on like two old friends that hadn't seen each other in ten years. Why were Max and Tom being so friendly?

It's not that I don't like Tom—I guess for a step-father, he's OK. He's good to my mother, and we live in his big fancy house, and he gives me money whenever I need it. He and Mom even have a baby now, Stephanie Arien Harris, and I *love* my new sister.

But just because I like him doesn't mean I'm going to be his friend, for heaven's sake. I like to keep a certain distance between us, if you know what I mean. I don't hug him or kiss him or even call him anything if I can help it. I love my *father*, who lives with Max in a condo. I feel sorry for my dad. I know he misses Mom and me.

But here Tom and Max were, in the library. And Max was saying, "Really? You'd let me have this stuff?"

Even that was strange. You see, Max is a true-blue, bona fide genius, and he should have been saying, "You would let me have this assortment of parapher-nalia?" I could tell he was really excited about some-thing because his vocabulary was slipping.

I stuck my head into the room to eavesdrop. "Sure," Tom answered. "I started this collection years ago, and it's grown quite a bit. But I know that now you'll need something special to call your own here

at this house. Besides, a young man of your intellec-
tual capacity should be kept stimulated."

Personally, I thought Max was mentally
*over*stimulated. At Dad's condo he has all kinds of
experiments, gerbils, a chemistry set, and rockets he
likes to launch from the beach. When Max is here at
Tom's house, he usually just sits around reading
encyclopedias. The kid should watch more TV.

But now Max was actually speechless with delight.
He just kept staring into the cardboard box Tom was
holding.

"What 'cha got there?" I asked, stepping into the
room. My curiosity had gotten the better of me.

"Oh, Cassie," Tom said, looking up. "Your mother
wants to talk to you. She's up in her room."

"OK." I shrugged. "So what's in the box?"

"My collection of oddities," Tom explained, nodding toward the box. "You're welcome to add to it,
too, Cassie."

"Can I label Max and stick him in there?" I teased.
"He's an oddity, for sure."

Max looked up and smiled. "Stop kidding, Cass.
Just look at this!"

He held up a perfectly ordinary unopened can of
Diet Coke.

"What's so great about that?" I asked. "Uncle

Jacob's got about fifty cans of Diet Coke in the kitchen."

"Not like this one," Max said, holding the can toward me. "Take it."

I took it, and it was empty! It was as light as a feather and totally empty.

"Where's the Coke?"

Max and Tom both snickered. What was this, a goofy conspiracy? "There's a tiny little hole, the size of a pinprick," Tom explained. "The Coke gradually leaked out. I kept the can as a conversation piece."

Max held up a blob of metal. "What do you think this is, Cass?"

I took the blob and held it. "I don't know. A paper-weight?"

"No." Tom shook his head. "It's a cow magnet."

"A cow *what?*"

"Cows have four stomachs," Tom explained. "Often when a calf is born, the farmer will make it swallow a magnet. Then when the cow eats nails, staples, tacks, wire, and other metal garbage, the stuff sticks to the magnet in the first stomach."

"That's gross!" I threw the metal blob back into the box.

Max laughed. "Actually, the magnet stays in the second stomach, the reticulum. When the cow is slaughtered, the metal is taken out and sold for scrap. Pretty neat, huh?"

"That's disgusting."

"Cassie, I think your mother would like to talk to you right away," Tom interrupted.

"OK," I muttered. "I'm going."

I left them as Tom was showing Max "a nose-picking instrument used by Tibetan women." I couldn't believe my brother was making friends with a man I had once considered my worst enemy.

I didn't go to Mom's room first, I went to my bedroom and threw my books on my bed and collapsed across it. Dribbles, my Chinese pug, scrambled on his little legs, trying to reach me. "Hi, Dribs," I muttered, reaching for him. "At least you missed me, right?"

He licked the side of my face and wiggled with excitement. "A girl's best friend is her dog," I whispered. "For sure."

It was nearly four o'clock, and Stephanie was probably awake from her nap. Coming home was nice these days, because Stephanie was a lot of fun to play with. She was old enough to sit up now, and it was fun to listen to her burble and laugh.

I tiptoed down the hall to Stephanie's nursery, right next to Mom and Tom's bedroom. The door was open, and I could hear the voices of my mother and Nick, my stepbrother. "Yes, we're going to teach you to ride a bike and swim," Nick said in singsongy baby talk.

My mom laughed. "Honestly, Nick, give her a chance to walk first, will you?" Her voice was warm and loving, and I could hear a smile in her voice. "You're going to spoil this baby to death."

"We all will," Nick answered. "I think she's really neat. Just don't expect me to, you know, kiss her or anything when my friends are around."

"I understand teenage boys," Mom said simply. "You don't have to worry, Nick. You won't even have to worry about being asked to baby-sit as long as Cassie is around. She loves playing with the baby, too."

From behind the cracked door, I made a horrible face. Was that all I was? Just a baby-sitter so Nick wouldn't ever have to do anything? He could be cool and macho with all his friends, and he'd never have to worry because Cassie will do all the dirty work.

I gritted my teeth and stomped back to my room. I made a vow—for at least one year, maybe two, I would *never* baby-sit Stephanie Arien Harris. Nick could do it. Or Tom. Or Mom. Or Max. Or even Uncle Jacob. But I wasn't going to cover for anyone.

I was not put on this earth simply to be a taken-for-granted baby-sitter.

Mom must have heard my stomping, because a few minutes later she knocked on my door and opened it. "Cassie, I have to talk to you," she said, not noticing that I was mad. She came in and sat down at my desk, then reached out to straighten the folds in my curtains. Uh oh. Whenever she took her time about saying something, it was usually bad news.

Finally she took a deep breath and turned to me. "Honey, your father has been transferred to Houston, and he has agreed that Max should live with us for the rest of the school year. In the summer and at Christmas, though, you and Max can go to Houston and spend time with him."

She cocked her head and smiled at me as if it were all so simple. I just stared at her. My dad was moving? When? Why?

"Why is he moving?" I blurted out. "When?"

"He's moving right away," Mom said. "Apparently he didn't want to cause any difficulties here in our home, and he was sure Max would adjust easily. Max will share Nick's room, and I'm sure they'll get along fine." She smiled again and waved her arms. "It's all working out so well I can't believe it."

"Why is he moving?" I asked again.

"I told you, NASA has transferred him from Cape Kennedy to Houston," Mom said, standing up. "It's a promotion, and he wants to go. He's already sold the condo, and he's moving tomorrow. I expect he'll come by tonight or tomorrow to say good-bye, so let's make it easy on him. OK, Cass?"

Mom patted my shoulder and left the room. I couldn't believe what she had just said. My father was moving halfway across the country, and she expected me to just act like it was no big deal, nothing out of the ordinary.

So that was why Tom was giving his precious weird collection to Max. It was a gift to make Max feel at home, and Max would take it and be happy. He and Nick would share a room, and they'd be best buddies in no time. But I didn't have anybody. My mother was busy with her new baby, and my father was moving a thousand miles away.

Everyone was happy at dinner except me. It would have been a blissful scene straight from Norman Rockwell, except that I sat there feeling like an outsider. Mom and Tom were at the end of the table spoon-feeding Stephanie mashed-up bits of their food. Max was busy explaining to Nick that people who have accidents on motorcycles have a 90 percent chance of injury or death, and people involved in car wrecks have only a 10 percent chance of being hurt or killed. Nick was listening intently, I knew, because he was planning to ask his dad for a new car on his sixteenth birthday.

Uncle Jacob was out for the evening; I think he had a date. After being at home all day, I guess he likes to get out, and I don't blame him. If I could, I'd get out, too. My food was dry and tasteless, and not even Stephanie's carrot-smeared face could cheer me up.

"May I be excused?" I muttered, pushing back my chair. "I've got homework to do."

"Not yet," Tom put down his napkin. "I've got a valentine surprise for your mom. A photographer is coming in a hour, and we're going to take a family picture. Cassie and Claire, you'll find new dresses hanging in the hall closet. Nick, put on your new dark suit, will you, and Max, there's a new suit for you in the hall closet, too."

Mom's eyes were shining. "Tom, how wonderful! But what about Stephanie?"

"I bought her a new little outfit covered with hearts," Tom said, bending his face toward the baby's. "She'll be her daddy's little sweetheart." He leaned forward and kissed Mom gently on the lips. "Happy Valentine's Day, honey."

I was about to ralph. (I don't know why I use that

word. Mom and Max use it, too. And everyone around here knows what it means. It sounds a lot nicer to yell "Ralph!" when you're carsick than to yell "I'm going to vomit!" Right?)

I left the table, and no one even noticed. In the hall closet I found my new dress. I have to admit it, Tom has good taste. It was red taffeta, with ruffles around the sleeves and a full skirt. It was probably very expensive, too, but I felt sad thinking that my dad must not have been able to afford anything like this for Valentine's Day. When it was just Mom, Dad, Max, and me, we were lucky if we got a valentine and candy for Valentine's Day.

Looking at the red dress, I thought of Sandy Shore and those red carnations. *I wonder which is worse, being happy when everyone around you thinks you're a miserable outsider or being a miserable outsider when everyone around you is happy?*

2

The photographer and his assistant came promptly at seven o'clock. "I'm glad you were on time," Mom told the lady assistant. "Stephanie gets fussy if we keep her up much later than eight."

"She's a darling baby," the lady said, jingling her car keys to keep Stephanie's attention. "I'm sure she'll photograph beautifully. You do want some shots of just the baby, don't you?"

"Of course."

So for half an hour we all sat in the library watching baby Stephanie giggle, squint, laugh, yawn, and cry as the photographer and the lady whooped and squeaked and made faces. I couldn't believe I had rushed to do my hair and makeup just to sit here and watch these pitiful people act like dummies in front of a baby.

"OK, let's set up for the family shot," the photographer said.

"I'll show you how to arrange the furniture," Mom offered. She glanced around at me. "Cassie, honey, will you hold Steffie?"

She didn't wait for an answer, she just thrust Stephanie toward me. If I hadn't put out my arms, the kid would have been on the floor.

Stephanie's big blue eyes watched me intently. "I know what you're thinking, kid," I whispered to her. "This *is* really dumb. I mean, who will care what we looked like on Valentine's Day? But sometimes you've got to humor the adults."

Stephanie actually laughed, and Mom looked up. "What did you do, Cass?" she asked. "You sure have a way with her."

I rolled my eyes and looked back at Stephanie. "We girls are going to have to stick together," I whispered again. "Max, Nick, and Tom—they're weird. I know Mom's a girl, but she's not thinking clearly right now. But you and me, kiddo, we'll make it through. OK?"

Who can understand what a baby is thinking? I thought she would laugh again, but she crinkled up her eyes and let out an ear-splitting scream. She didn't stop, either, and Mom shook her head disgustedly. "Nick, honey, will you take the baby? We've just got to get her quiet or this picture will be ruined."

Nick took Stephanie from me without a word, and I felt completely humiliated. What did I do? I couldn't help it that the baby cried. It wasn't my fault if this dumb picture had a screaming baby in it.

Nick jostled Stephanie gently up and down and sang "You Ain't Nothing But a Hound Dog," which somehow made her stop crying.

The lady assistant looked at Mom and said, "You have a great group of kids."

Mom smiled and said, "Yes, we're very fortunate. We really are one big, happy family."

I was going to ralph. I bit my lip and ran into the kitchen.

"Cassie," Mom called from the library. Her voice was impatient. "We're ready now. What are you doing?"

"Just getting a drink," I called back. "I'm thirsty." The truth was, I didn't think I could stand being in that room one more minute. I closed my eyes and wished with all my heart that Max and I were home with Dad in his condo. At least we were *part* of a happy family. But no, my father was leaving for Houston, and he hadn't even come to say good-bye. I was stuck here, in this house, where that happy family stuff was a lie. I was an outsider and I was not happy.

The coffeepot was on the stove, about half-full of leftover cold coffee. Without stopping to think, I picked it up and poured it over the front of my dress. It stained the brilliant red a deep brown and puddled on the floor.

"Cassie!" Mom stood in the doorway. "What on earth?"

"I had an accident," I mumbled. "I was thirsty and saw this coffee and accidentally spilled it . . ."

"You don't even *like* coffee!" Mom shrieked. "You did that on purpose!"

I couldn't answer her. I just stood there with my eyes full of angry tears, hating myself, hating this red dress, hating this family.

Tom appeared in the doorway. "What happened?" He was honestly puzzled.

"Cassie's done it again," Mom snapped, and I wondered vaguely what she meant by "again." This was the first time I had ever poured coffee on myself. "She obviously doesn't want to be a part of this picture."

"It wouldn't be a family picture without Cass," Tom said. "She can put on another dress."

"My name is Cassie," I said as smoothly as I could. "Only my mom and Max call me Cass."

Tom shook his head. "Aren't we past that defensiveness now, Cassie? Come on. Go upstairs, change, and come back down so we can take the picture. Hurry now," he said, smiling. "I'm paying these people by the hour."

"No," Mom said. "Tom, she doesn't want to be in the picture, that's obvious. Let's take it without her. It will be fine."

"Claire, I think I should handle this," Tom said, looking down at Mom. "I think Cassie will come around."

"I don't want her in this picture," Mom said, her voice quivering in anger. She was really, really upset.

"I'm going upstairs," I answered. "And you don't have to put me in the picture. Don't worry about it. My feelings won't be hurt one bit."

My mom was so angry with me she wrote me a note. I guess she couldn't trust herself to talk to me in person, and apparently she and Tom still disagreed over the whole thing, so she couldn't ask him to yell at me.

She must have slipped the note under my door while I was asleep because I found it on the floor the next morning:

Dear Cass:
You will never know how you hurt me last night. Not only did you insult your stepfather and your entire family, but you showed nothing but complete and total self-centeredness. You were not thinking of me, or Tom, or even Nick,

Max, and Stephanie, who might have enjoyed that picture for years to come. No. Instead, you pouted when Tom was nice enough to buy you a beautiful dress. You were upset when he was thoughtful. You were cruel and mean and, as I think you would put it, snotty.

Sometime today, after things have cooled down, you will owe me and Tom an apology. If you can give it, I can forgive you. But honestly, Cassie, sometimes I feel I don't even know you anymore. Worse yet, I don't see how you can go to church and pretend to be so spiritual when you treat your family like this. You've become totally self-centered.

Think about it.

Mom

My face turned red as I read her letter. It hurt that my mother would say those things. It *really* hurt that she thought I was just pretending at church. I was trying to be the best Christian I could be, but my own mother thought I was cruel and mean and snotty. Was I?

I climbed back into bed and buried my head under my pillow. I felt numb and I couldn't even cry. I could see why she thought I was ungrateful— to her it must have looked like I just didn't like Tom.

But that was only part of it. Why couldn't she see what I was feeling?

Maybe she was right. Maybe I had become self-centered. Maybe I should try to do something to prove that I wasn't a total snob. But what?

I slipped off my bed and onto my knees. "Oh God, I've really blown it this time," I whispered. "I know you know what I was feeling, but my mother sure doesn't understand. Please help me work this out. Please don't let this happen again. Show me what to do, please, God."

Dribbles tugged on my nightgown; he had to go outside. I scooped him up in my arms and stood up. One more thought occurred to me, and I reminded the Lord: "It would help, God, if I could prove that I'm not self-centered."

3

I was still trying to find a way to prove I wasn't totally self-centered at lunch on Monday. I was thinking so hard about my problem, in fact, that Chip gave up trying to talk to me, and Andrea and Eric hardly glanced in my direction.

Andrea wouldn't be any help, anyway. Her problems are completely ordinary, and mine aren't. Her parents aren't divorced. She wouldn't understand what it's like to be torn between your mom and dad. Plus, since Mom and I moved from our old house into Tom's house, I don't see Andrea as much as I used to. So she has no idea what's going on in my life. Besides, now that Andrea's going with Eric Brandt, whom I can't stand, she's been giving me the cold shoulder.

I thought we would be best friends forever. I guess time changes things, though. Now the only really good friend I have is Chip. It's funny. I used to be in love with him—I mean, I got all shaky and scared when he came by, and all goose-pimply if he talked to me. But we've become so close now he seems more like a brother. Time has changed things with him, too, just like with Andrea. But I think in Chip's case, the change is for the better.

"Cassie? Are you going to be spaced out all day?" Chip's voice brought me back to reality.

"Sorry. I was just thinking."

"Problems at home?" Chip knew all about my struggles with Tom Harris and company.

"Sort of. Last night I poured coffee all over a new dress Tom gave me."

Chip shrugged. "So? Anyone can spill coffee."

"I didn't spill it, I poured it." I leaned forward and whispered: "And when I poured the coffee on it, I was *in* the dress!"

"No way! You're not totally crazy, are you?"

"Not yet." I smiled at him, grateful for his clear blue eyes. Sometimes I think all the brown-eyed people in the world (like Tom, Max, Nick, Dad, and even Dribbles) are out to make my life complicated. But there are always people like Chip and Steffie, with clear blue eyes, that remind me there are other people in the world, after all.

"You're drifting again."

"Sorry." I finished my carton of milk and neatly tucked the straw inside. "I need a project, Chip."

"For science?"

"No, just for me. I want to prove to my mom that I'm not totally self-centered."

Chip thought a moment. "That's easy. Just go home and do something for her. Wash the dishes, vacuum the floors, or something like that."

"I can't. Uncle Jacob has all that stuff done by the time I get home. Besides, that's too easy."

"Offer to baby-sit so she and Tom can have an evening out."

I gritted my teeth. "Absolutely not."

Chip leaned back. "Ouch! Sore spot, huh? OK, I give up. You'll have to think of something yourself."

"OK," I answered, picking up my tray. "I will."

Our biology class went to the library for research on our term science projects. As we filed in, groups of kids fanned past me and headed in little groups to the study tables. I hung back. I was in no mood to sit with Andrea and Eric Brandt.

Blakely Russo walked in alone and every guy in the room noticed her. She is gorgeous, and I mean turn-around-for-a-second-look beautiful. She has light brown hair with golden highlights, her figure is perfect, and her eyes are so wide they seem to take up half her face. She has flawless skin and sophisticated clothes, and she carries herself like a princess. Every girl I know hates her.

Blakely Russo sat at a table by herself, and I thought about sitting with her, but I figured I'd just feel like a dwarf sitting next to Snow White. The only other available seat in our section was at a table where Sandy Shore sat hunched over a stack of encyclopedia volumes.

I walked over and put my books down across the table from her. "Hi," I whispered. "Can I sit here?"

She looked up, a faint expression of surprise on her face. "Sit here?" she asked.

"Yes. Is this seat taken?"

Sandy shook her head. "No."

I sat down and pulled out my notebook and glanced over at Sandy. I couldn't believe it, but she was wearing one of the valentine carnations pinned to the collar of the shirt underneath today's tent dress.

"That's a pretty flower," I whispered, trying to be nice. "Red is one of my favorite colors."

Sandy didn't even look up, but I saw her smile. She hesitated a moment, then reached into a book and pulled out a little card. I recognized it as one of the gift cards from the Junior Class Flower Sale.

"Look at that," she said, holding the card up.

I read it in a whisper. Someone had scrawled, "Sandy Shore, Sandy Shore, you're the one we all adore. Love, Elmer Potsinjammer."

"There is no Elmer Potsinjammer," I whispered back. "Not at this school, anyway."

"I know," Sandy whispered. "I checked in the office." She took the card and gently placed it back in her book.

I was confused. What was I supposed to do? Did she want me to congratulate her, or had she realized it was all a terrible joke? Maybe one of her parents had explained it to her—

"What do you think about that?" I asked. "I mean, I'd be dying to know who sent me flowers and why."

Sandy looked directly at me for the first time, and I was surprised because I don't think I had ever been this close to her. She had dark, brilliant eyes and thick lashes without a trace of mascara on them. Her skin was paler than typing paper, but now her cheeks were tinged faintly with pink.

"I think I know why they sent me the flowers," she said simply. "But I enjoyed them anyway. No one had ever sent me flowers before, and no one had ever written me a poem. It almost made me glad to have my horrible name."

"You don't like your name?" This was news to me.

"My name is Sandra Cheryl Shore," she said. "I was named after two aunts. My dad thought it would be a tremendous joke if my name could read

'Sandy C. Shore.' But everyone who really knows me calls me Sandra."

"Sandra." It sounded dignified. "I know what you mean," I whispered. "My father named me Cassiopeia, after the constellation. Everyone calls me Cassie, except, of course, for my family. They call me Cass."

Sandy—I mean, Sandra—didn't say anything. She just nodded and went back to reading her book.

But a flash of inspiration hit me. Here, right under my nose, was my opportunity to help someone. I could help my classmates and friends meet Sandra Cheryl Shore. I would, and could, make her presentable. All she had to do was drop a few pounds, wash and style her hair, put on a little makeup, get a little sun, and buy a few clothes. In time, things would change. I could give Sandra Shore a new life. I was sure God would want me to do this. Best of all, it would help me prove to everyone at home that I was not a snobby, self-centered person.

I didn't realize I was studying Sandy, but she obviously felt my gaze and looked up. There was a shadow of irritation across her brow. "Aren't you going to work on your project?" she asked, pointing toward my science book.

"Y-y-yes," I stammered. "Right now. And Sandra, how about meeting me after school by my locker?

It's number 1212. I have an idea I'd like to discuss with you."

"I don't know." She looked at me suspiciously.

"You won't regret it," I whispered. "It'll be the best project ever."

"OK, for a few minutes. Then I have to get home."

Sandy went back to her work, and I had to force myself to think about science for the next hour. My brain kept racing ahead to what would be the greatest transformation since the first caterpillar emerged from its cocoon.

4

Sandy was waiting for me by my locker. She looked a little nervous, standing alone in the hall, and she breathed a sigh of relief when I came up. "I thought you forgot," she said simply.

"No." I shook my head. "I just had to say good-bye to Chip."

She smiled a little half-smile. "He's your boy-friend?"

I shrugged. "I guess so. He's my best friend."

"He seems really nice."

I shifted my books in my arms. I really hadn't thought much about how to ask Sandy to volunteer to become my make-over project. I didn't want to make her feel bad, but I was sure she needed help. After all, she was a mess, and she had to know it, right?

I took a breath and plunged in. "Sandy, you know there's a Spring Fling for the sophomore class in April, right?"

She nodded. "So?"

"So, would you like to go?"

She looked at me like I'd suggested she fly to Mars next Thursday. "No, I don't think so."

"Come on! I've been thinking about you, and if it's OK with you, I'd like to, uh, try out some ideas I've had with clothes, makeup, and hairstyle. I've been doing some new exercises, too, and I thought we could do these things together and sort of get in shape for the Spring Fling. I'll bet I could even get you a date."

Sandy shook her head and took a step away from me. "I don't like parties," she said, "and I hate to exercise. Thanks a lot, but I've got to go home."

"What's your hurry?" I asked, taking big steps to keep up with her.

"'Leave It to Beaver' is on at four o'clock," she said simply. "It's my favorite show."

It was obvious she'd rather be left alone, but I just knew I could win her over if she'd only give me a chance. We were just walking out the doors of the building when I decided to try what Max calls "reverse psychology."

"Say, Sandy, I mean, Sandra," I caught myself, "to tell you the truth, I could really use a friend right now. You see, Andrea and I used to be best friends, but since I moved I don't see her as much anymore. And Chip helps his uncle, who's a vet, after school.

So I only see him at church and in a couple of classes. My brother Max—well, he's a brother. Besides, I really miss having a girlfriend to talk to. Don't you?"

Sandy squinted as the bright sunlight hit her eyes. "I've never really had a girlfriend," she said, "but I have a big sister, and we're very close. You know my sister, don't you?"

I didn't know Meredith Shore, but I had heard about her. She was president of the Senior Class, in the National Honor Society, and on practically every committee the school offered. She wasn't a raving beauty, but she looked sharp and seemed very intelligent and hardworking. She and Sandy were about as opposite as two people could be.

"I know about Meredith," I said, still keeping up. "But you still need a friend your own age, Sandy. Come on, let's do this together."

Sandy didn't say anything, but she stopped walking. "I don't need you to walk me home," she said simply. "I'd rather walk alone."

I never thought it would be this hard to help someone. Maybe pure and simple honesty would work. "OK, I'll be honest," I said, stopping on the sidewalk and facing Sandy. "My mom and I had a big fight the other night, and she thinks I'm totally self-centered. I thought the best way to show her I'm not would be to help someone else. I want to help you, if you'll let me. If not," I said, shrugging, "well, OK. Whatever you want to do."

Sandy looked at me steadily, then said, "I didn't think you really wanted to be my friend. No one does."

"But they will," I said, squeezing her arm. "I think we can get you shaped up so that people won't pre-judge you by the way you look. No one even knows the person that's inside you."

Sandy looked down at the ground and nodded. "OK," she said. "I'll go along with this until the Spring Fling. But you can't push me, and if I want out, you have to leave me alone."

"Deal." I held out my hand, and she shyly shook it.

I spun on my heel and ran toward the parking lot where my ride was waiting. "I'll see you tomorrow," I called to her. "Meet me by the gym in the morn-ing. I'll write up our plan of action tonight."

Things were really going to be great. How hard could this be? Sandy Shore was going to thank me forever when we were finished.

Tom and Max were waiting for me in the parking lot. Brother. I was ten minutes late. My dad always hated it when I was late. He'd gripe and complain that time was life and tell me that by being late, I'd wasted ten minutes of Max's life and ten minutes of his, and that twenty minutes of something as irreplaceable as life was a terrible waste indeed.

But Tom didn't seem at all concerned that I was late. He was reading the *Wall Street Journal* and hardly even looked up when I opened the car door. "Is that you, Cass?" he mumbled from behind the newspaper pages.

"Yes." I climbed in and settled my books in my lap. "Sorry I'm late."

"No problem."

Max was in the backseat reading *There Is No Zoo in Zoology and Other Beastly Mispronunciations,* and he glanced up only to say, "Did you know that *often* is correctly pronounced *awf*-en? You shouldn't say the *t.*"

"That's great, Max." Max went back to his book, and Tom sat there for three or four more minutes reading his paper while I fidgeted. What was he doing? He was wasting my life, Max's life, his life—

He finally put the paper down. "Wanted to finish that article," he said. "There's an interesting law case going on in New York involving a woman who is suing a department store."

If my dad was thinking about something, he'd just blurt it out whether you wanted to hear it or not. But Tom was obviously waiting for me to ask,

"What is she suing them for?" and I didn't want to ask. I leaned my head back on the seat and closed my eyes. Maybe he'd think I had a headache.

Tom started the car and cleared his throat. "Seems the woman was hit on the head by a piece of falling lumber. She used to be able to hypnotize herself so that she could undergo surgery without anesthetic, but now she says she can't."

I stayed quiet. Max wasn't listening, he was absorbed in his book.

Tom went on, a little halfheartedly. He probably was wishing he could trade us in for stepkids with more personality.

"She's suing because she says she lost psychic abilities," Tom mumbled. "Can you imagine?"

"Can we hurry?" I asked. "I've got a lot of homework to get done tonight."

"Sure." Tom put his foot on the accelerator, and we sped home without another word from either of us.

5

Sandy was waiting for me outside the gym just like I'd told her to. She looked perfectly horrible, and I wished I'd brought my mother's Polaroid, so I could snap a "before" picture. The worse she looked now, the better she'd look after my project.

"Hi," I said, pulling the gym door open for her. "Isn't it a beautiful day?"

Sandy squinted toward the sky. "Is it? I didn't notice."

"It's perfect," I said, following her into the gym. "Just like you're going to be, Sandra Cheryl Shore. Just wait and see."

There was a big scale outside the gym teacher's office. I don't think anyone ever uses it, except maybe the wrestlers, but it was perfect for Sandy's morning weigh-ins. No one else was around, the scales were accurate, and Sandy could face the day with encouragement when she watched the pounds roll off every morning.

I put my books on the floor and pointed to the

scale. "We'll weigh you in every morning," I said. "That way you'll have motivation to stick to your diet, and you'll be changing before your eyes."

"My diet?" Sandy asked, staring at the scale. "You didn't say anything about a diet."

"It's the only way to lose weight," I said. "But you'll only have to diet for a little while, I promise. So get on the scale, and let's see what your starting weight will be."

Sandy didn't budge. She just stared at the scale. "I weigh about 140," she said finally. "I weighed myself this morning at home."

I shook my head. "These scales are more accurate than bathroom scales," I told her. "We'll have a better picture with these."

"Well, I'll weigh myself. You don't have to watch," Sandy said, still not moving.

"It's OK, Sandy. What do you think I'll do, tell everyone? I want to keep track of your progress, and I have to know what you weigh now."

She closed her eyes, not even willing to look at the scales. "You won't just take my word for it?"

I pretended to be mad. "Sandra Cheryl Shore, get on these scales!" I snapped, pointing to the platform. "Right now!"

Sandy slowly put down her books and slipped off her shoes. "Remember that clothes weigh at least a pound," she said. Then she stepped on the platform and covered her eyes with her fingers.

The scale's balance clunked downward. "OK," I said, fingering the weights. "Let's see how much you weigh."

I moved the heavy bottom weight to 100, and the balance didn't budge. I moved the heavy bottom weight to 150, and it still didn't move. Sandy was wrong about one thing—she didn't weigh 140.

I gently moved the smaller top weight: 151, 152, 153 . . . I slid it over to 159 and the balance finally began to move . . . 160—

"You weigh 160," I announced, pulling out my spiral notebook.

"Take a pound off," Sandy said, stepping off the platform. She slipped into her shoes. "Remember clothes weigh at least a pound."

"Let's just stay consistent and go by the scale, OK?" I told her. "No matter what clothes you're wearing."

Sandy didn't look happy, but she picked up her books. "Now what?"

I shrugged. "Don't eat anything fattening, OK? At lunch, have a salad with no dressing. Drink diet Coke only. And water. My mom drinks lots of water when she's dieting. For supper, have another salad and a slice of diet bread for a treat."

"That's all?"

"Sure. You want to lose weight fast, don't you? And tonight, do some exercises—either a hundred situps or jump rope for five or ten minutes. Run around the block, or even walk. But you need to do something active for at least twenty minutes."

"Can I have a snack?"

"No." I looked at her closely. Somehow I didn't think her heart was in this diet.

The gym door opened, and Blakely Russo walked toward us. "Come on, Sandra," I said, pulling her by the arm.

After Blakely had passed us, I whispered, "You could look as good as she does, you know. All you have to do is exert yourself and have a little discipline. You can do it."

Sandy turned and watched Blakely step on the same scales we had been using. "Do you think *she* goes on diets?" she asked.

"No, but she watches her weight," I answered. "Like you've got to do. OK?"

Sandy looked back at me and nodded. "OK. It'll probably be impossible, but I'll try."

"Just one more thing. I want you to eat lunch with me and Chip. That way I can help you resist temptation. I'm going to help you, Sandra. You're not going to be in this alone."

Sandy nodded and walked past me on her way to her locker, but I caught a glimpse of something in her eyes that looked like fear. I was going to help her find a new life, so what was she afraid of?

Chip, Andrea, Eric, and I were at the lunch table before Sandy appeared. I pulled over an extra chair, and Andrea asked, "Who's that for?"

"A surprise." I smiled. Like everyone else, they would be amazed at the difference in Sandy Shore and even more amazed that I had helped pull off the greatest change in the history of Astronaut High School.

"Look!" I heard a freshman boy squeal behind me. "It's Tons-of-fun! She's eating in the cafeteria today!"

"Oh no!" his friend answered. "There won't be anything left for anyone else."

I glanced up. Sandy was coming out of the cafeteria line with her tray, and she was close enough to hear everything the boys were saying. I glared over at them, but they were too busy giggling at their own cleverness to notice me.

"Uh oh," Andrea muttered. "Here comes the beached whale. Don't look up, anyone, and maybe she'll leave. Good grief, she's coming right this way!"

"I invited her," I said smoothly. I smiled and waved my hand. "Sandra! Over here!"

"Are you crazy?" Andrea hissed. "Have you gone nuts?"

Even Chip seemed puzzled, and Eric was doubled over in laughter. I lowered my voice so Sandy wouldn't hear. "Hush, all of you. I'm trying to be her friend, and I'm helping her go on a diet."

"A diet?" Eric howled. "Cassie Perkins, you're not a miracle worker."

Sandy stood next to the empty chair, her face red. "Hi," she said simply. "Maybe I should go eat outside. There's a tree out there, and lots of shade."

"No, Sandra, you can join us." I pulled out the chair.

Her eyes were pleading with me. "Please, I'd rather eat outside."

I was torn. I didn't really want to leave my friends, but I had promised Sandy I'd stick by her. I couldn't really expect her to stay in the cafeteria when the people at my own table were making fun of her.

"Sure, eating under the tree sounds nice," I said. "And it's just for one day, right?" I looked around the table. "Does anyone want to join us?"

Andrea snickered and looked away. Eric looked at Andrea, about to burst with laughter. Chip really didn't understand what I was doing, but I knew he'd come if I insisted.

"It's OK, Chip," I said, letting him off the hook.

"Sandra and I wanted to eat alone today. I'll see you later."

I picked up my tray and followed Sandy outside, but I could hear Andrea say, "What's this *Sandra* stuff? What on earth is she up to, Chip? Has Cassie joined the ugly club?"

Sandy had a point. Under this huge oak tree on the school lawn there was a bench perfect for eating lunch. We sat down and put our trays between us. I lifted up my special cafeteria cheeseburger and took a bite while Sandy picked at her salad.

"I feel like a rabbit," she said, munching on lettuce. "Maybe I'll turn into one if I eat enough of this stuff."

"Lettuce has practically no calories," I said, wiping a dribble of grease from my chin. "And carrots are good for you, too. Just don't put any cheese or bacon or dressing or nuts on your salad. And no salt."

"Why not?" Sandy asked.

I shrugged. "I don't know. That's just what my mom does when she diets. She just had a baby, you know, and she lost her weight in no time at all. She does aerobics three or four times a week, and she and my stepfather walk a lot after dinner."

Sandy crunched a carrot; I ate my brownie. She

drank a cup of water; I slurped the last bit of my chocolate milk with my straw and then moved my tray out of the way.

I reached for my notebook and pencil. "I figure you need to lose thirty-six pounds," I said. "If you're five-foot, six-inches tall and weighed four pounds for each inch over five feet, that'd be 124 pounds. Let's make that your goal weight."

Sandy made a face. "How'd you figure that out?"

"My brother's a genius. He knows all kinds of stuff like this. Now, if you need to lose thirty-six pounds in seven weeks, that would be about five pounds per week you would need to lose."

I chewed on the end of my pencil. "I don't think you can lose that much. My mom says you shouldn't try to lose more than two or three pounds per week, or you might get sick."

"I take vitamins," Sandy offered. "They'll help."

"Maybe. But maybe we should just aim to have you lose three pounds a week."

"Five. I want to lose five."

It was the first time she had shown any real excitement, and I didn't want to dampen her spirits. "Four. We'll compromise. No more than four pounds per week."

Sandy shrugged. "But if I lose more, that'll be OK."

"Agreed. So by the Spring Fling, you should weigh somewhere around 132 pounds."

Sandy's eyes began to glow. "I'd lose a dress size," she said. "Maybe two. I could fit into a new dress, maybe I could even get new shoes. . . ."

"With a new hairdo and new makeup . . ."

"And earrings to match . . ."

"And Poison perfume . . ."

Sandy giggled. "I can't believe it. Do you think it will really work?"

"Sure," I said, standing up. "You've just had a good, low-calorie lunch. How do you feel?"

Sandy put her hand on her stomach and cocked her head as if listening to her body. "I feel fine," she said. "Even kind of full. I think I can last until supper without a snack."

"Good. Now remember, I won't be there at supper, so eat a salad, drink lots of water, and think thin! I'll meet you tomorrow morning, and we'll weigh in again."

"OK!"

6

Sandy was eager to get on the scales the next morning. She kept her eyes shut tight while I moved the top weight: 156, 157 . . . "One hundred fifty-seven and a half pounds!" I announced.

Sandy opened her eyes wide in surprise. "Really? I lost three pounds in one day? Goodness, at this rate, I can lose my thirty-six pounds in—" She counted on her fingers. "Twelve days!"

"It doesn't work that way," I said. "You always lose weight fast at first, because it's really excess water weight. So, how do you feel?"

"I feel good," Sandy said, her eyes shining. "I even feel skinnier."

"What did you eat yesterday?"

Sandy thought. "A salad for lunch, a salad for dinner, a slice of whole wheat bread, and about two gallons of water." She grinned widely and I noticed that she had a really pretty smile. I'd never seen her smile like that before.

"Are you hungry?"

"No," she said quickly, then she looked away and smiled. "Well, last night in bed I was so hungry I thought I'd die. I almost got up to raid the refrigerator, but I thought about weighing in this morning and changed my mind."

"Good for you!" I pulled out my notebook and wrote the date and Sandy's current weight. "Now today, try to eat the same thing—just salads, no dressing, and lots of water."

"I'm so excited I might even skip dinner," Sandy said. "Maybe tomorrow I'll lose four pounds."

"Slow and steady, Sandy," I warned her.

"It's OK," she said, slipping into her shoes. "I've been taking extra vitamins."

That afternoon I was in home ec when the intercom interrupted our class. "Mrs. Jenkins, could you please send Cassie Perkins to the office?" the secretary asked.

"Yes, I will," Mrs. Jenkins answered. She looked at me. "You're wanted," she said.

A collective *oooooh* came up from the other girls. "What did you do, Cassie?" Christine Miller asked. "You've got to be in trouble."

"Maybe I've been chosen as student of the month," I answered, gathering my purse and books. "You never know."

I wasn't student of the month. The secretary pointed me toward the school clinic without a word, and through the door, I could see Sandy Shore laid out on a bed, her skin pale and sweaty. "What happened?" I asked the nurse.

"Are you Cassie Perkins?" she snapped. I nodded. "I don't know what you're trying to do," she said, her dark brows rushing together. "But this girl cannot live on one salad a day. I don't know where you girls get your ideas, but fad diets can kill you."

"I didn't tell her to eat one salad a day," I tried to defend myself. "I'm just trying to help her watch what she eats."

"You're no medical expert," the nurse said. "And you don't understand heavy people. They have a different metabolism than you do. If she wants to lose weight, she should do it under a doctor's care. Fad diets don't work, and starvation diets will hurt you."

I walked over to Sandy, and her eyelashes fluttered open. "What happened, Sandra?" I asked.

"I just got weak in history class," she said. "I think I fainted."

"You'll be OK," I told her. "Go home and eat a good dinner. Get your strength back. I'll figure out what to do from here."

"Is the deal off?"

I was tempted to forget the entire thing. I had

been too disorganized, and I was no doctor. Maybe putting Sandy on a diet was a terrible idea. "I'll go home and think this through," I told her. "Don't worry. I'll consult an expert and have an answer tomorrow."

"You know an expert?" Sandy muttered. Her voice was still weak.

"My brother's an expert on everything," I told her. "I'll talk to Max tonight. In the meantime, though, you ought to ask your mother for a doctor's appointment. Between the doctor and Max, I know we can work this out."

I told Max about my problem in the car while Tom listened. *Nosy of him,* I thought, but I guess he couldn't help hearing. "So I need to know how and what Sandy should be eating," I told Max. "Can you come up with something tonight?"

"I'll look into it," Max told me, his dark eyes serious. "I think there's a national health data base I can access tonight."

"What's this girl's name, Cassie?" Tom asked, his eyes on the road. "Did you say her last name was Beach?"

"Shore." What was the matter with him? If he was going to eavesdrop on my conversations, he could at least get the details straight.

"I used to know a salesman named Shore a few years ago," Tom said. "He sold burglar alarms to several businesses in the block where we have our law office. Turned out he never intended to put in the alarms. He just skipped town with the money."

"I don't think it's the same family," I said. "I don't think Sandy's father is a crook."

Tom shrugged and kept driving. What nerve! I was glad Sandy wasn't in the car to hear Tom accuse her father of being a thief. Imagine a man leaving town with the money that was supposed to be spent on an alarm to protect people from thieves!

I leaned my head against the window. It was bad enough when a father like mine left town for a perfectly good reason, if he left without even saying good-bye to his daughter. Still, Dad must have had a good reason for not coming by. I was sure he'd tell me, too, when he called. As soon as he was settled in, he'd call and we'd talk. My dad wouldn't let me down.

The phone rang that night, and I dove to answer it. Nick beat me to it, though, and just looked at me as if I were nuts for sprawling across the floor in such a rush. He listened for a minute then hung up the phone. "It's for Mom," he said. "She picked it up upstairs."

I buried my face in the carpet, and Nick stepped

over me and plopped his long body into a wing chair. "Who are you expecting a call from?" he asked. "Chip? Or your dad?"

I closed my eyes, glad that Nick couldn't see my face in the carpet. Of all the people in this house, Nick was the only one who even noticed that I was upset because Dad didn't come to say good-bye. Mom and Tom had forgotten all about it, and Max hadn't stopped to think. Besides, Dad told Max good-bye at the condo. But no one said anything to me until it was too late.

"I'm not expecting a call from anybody," I said, turning my face to the wall. "I just like hurtling furniture for fun."

Nick didn't say anything right away. "It's OK, Cassie, I understand, or at least I think I do," he finally said. "I tried to imagine how I would feel if my dad moved away and I didn't get to see him. I'd be pretty upset, too."

"I'm OK," I said, more firmly.

"Good." Nick said, clicking the television remote control so that the channels flipped by endlessly. "Just don't take it out on my dad, OK? He's really trying, Cassie, but you're not giving him a chance."

What did Nick know? I got up without looking at him and went upstairs to my room.

7

I knocked on Max's door with the usual amount of caution. You never knew what living, creeping, slimy thing could come out of his room. But when I pushed the door open, Max was sitting calmly at his computer and wearing his headphones. He was wearing one of his favorite outfits, a cast-off lab coat that Dad had given him.

I pulled one of the earphones away from his ear. "Are you finished with that stuff I asked you to get?"

Max looked up. "I have an entire file for you," he said, pointing to a manila folder on the floor. "Let me finish this, and I'll explain it all to you."

Max's computer had run off a stack of articles. I flipped through them: "How to Eat for More Energy," "How to Fat-Proof Your Child," "Quick Tips from Diet Doctors," "The No-Diet Slim Down," and "When Your Child Is Overweight."

"I don't have time to read all this stuff," I told Max. "Can't you boil it down for me? Sandy needs my help tomorrow."

"It's basically pretty simple," Max said, pushing some buttons on his computer. Something in the big metal box whirred, and his printer began spitting out more paper. "What you have to do, Cassie, is convince Sandy that she's *not* on a diet."

"Not on a diet? Then how is she going to lose any weight?"

Max shook his head. "The very word *diet* seems to imply that when she's reached a certain weight, she'll come off the 'diet.' If she does that, she'll just regain all the weight she loses."

"But," I said, holding up a finger to get his attention, "she'll be thin for the Spring Fling. That's what's important."

"That's a bad attitude." Max took a deep breath, and I settled back for a lecture. "You see, in order to really change her life, you have to change her eating habits forever, not just for a little while. She needs to learn to eat healthy foods in a healthy way. If she learns to do that, the excess weight will come off and stay off. It's a slower way to go, but the change is permanent."

The printer stopped zipping out paper, and Max reached for the printed sheet. "I've entered Sandy's age, height, present weight, and goal weight into this program," he explained. "And this is a breakdown of what Sandy should eat every day."

I looked at the page:

Sandy Age: 14 Height: 5'6" Weight: 160 Goal: 124

Calories:	1200	Vitamin B1:	1.1 mg
Protein:	36 g	Vitamin B2:	1.3 mg
Carbohydrate:	174 g	Niacin:	14 mg
Total Fat:	40 g	Vitamin B6:	2 mg
Saturated Fat:	12 g	Vitamin B12:	3 mcg
Cholesterol:	120 mg	Folacin:	400 mcg
Dietary Fiber:	28 g	Sodium:	1200 mg
Caffeine:	200 mg	Calcium:	1000 mg
Vitamin A:	4000 IU	Magnesium:	300 mg
Vitamin C:	60 mg	Potassium:	5625 mg
Vitamin D:	400 IU	Iron:	18 mg
Vitamin E:	8 mg	Zinc:	15 mg

"Basically," Max explained as I read, "she should lose no more than two pounds per week. If she eats according to this schedule, she'll reach her goal weight in eighteen weeks. That's pretty good."

"Eighteen weeks?" I stopped to figure in my head. "That's nearly five months! That would take forever!"

"No, it won't," Max said. "And five months of steady weight loss will keep her healthy, and she'll feel good. Crash dieting will only make her miserable and sick, and she'll probably regain every ounce she loses plus even more weight."

I shoved the paper back to Max. "I don't understand this. How do caffeine and fiber translate into hamburgers and french fries? We could count her calories, but I have no idea how many vitamins are in certain foods."

"The computer can do it," Max explained. "If Sandy will just count her calories and write down everything she eats, I can put her food logs into the computer and get a printout of how well she's doing. She can adjust the next day if she's not on target. Plus, if she takes vitamins, they will make up any deficiencies not covered in her diet."

"She's taking vitamins." I nodded, glad to see that we were at least doing something right. "She's even taking *extra* vitamins."

"No!" Max sighed and shook his head as if I were a very stupid child. "Too many vitamins can be dangerous. If it's a daily vitamin pill, she should take one and only one. A calcium supplement might be a good idea if she doesn't drink milk, but that's it. Nothing else. She needs to eat good healthy food: vegetables, fruits, potatoes, and whole wheat bread."

"Potatoes? I thought potatoes were fattening."

"It's only the butter and sour cream that people put on potatoes that are fattening," Max answered. "You would have to eat eleven pounds of potatoes to put on one pound of weight. A potato has no more calories than an apple."

He crinkled his nose. "Food is fascinating. Did you know your body burns more calories to eat a stalk of celery than the celery has in it?" He laughed. "You could lose a lot of weight by eating nothing but celery."

"But you'd be sick, right?" I reminded him. "That sounds pretty unhealthy to me, not to mention disgusting. I hate celery."

"You ought to learn to like it. Our bodies are designed to run on certain kinds of food, and they perform best when we feed them the right things. It's amazing that they run at all when we stuff them with junk." Max turned back to his computer. "Did you know the average person eats about a *ton* of food and drink a year? But we don't weigh a ton. Our bodies burn off the fuel. So if your friend will exercise, she'll lose weight even faster."

"Thanks," I said, gathering up the folder and the stack of articles. "But I'm going to have a hard time just getting her to count calories."

"Well, remind her to keep a food log of everything she eats," Max said, turning back to his computer. "Make sure she's honest. I think this will be an interesting study."

The next morning Sandy met me by the gym, and we weighed her in. "One fifty-eight," I told her. "That's not too bad considering you ate last night, right?"

Sandy nodded and slipped back into her loafers.

"My mom and dad took me to the doctor," she said, rubbing her nose. Her eyes shifted away from mine. "And he said whatever you wanted to do was fine."

"OK." I looked down at Max's stack of papers. "Well, there's a lot here to go over, but basically I want you just to write down everything you eat today, OK? Everything. And Max says to take one and only one vitamin a day, plus a calcium supplement, if you can. And you need to bring in the vitamin label so he can enter it into his computer."

Sandy's eyebrow shot up. She was impressed. I felt pretty proud of my kid brother. "Max says we should aim only for two pounds a week and that you should eat twelve hundred calories a day. I brought this calorie-counting book for you to use. It lists practically every food and tells you how many calories it has."

Sandy took the book and tossed it in her book bag. "Anything else?"

"Yes. Let's meet this afternoon and read through some of these articles together, OK? I think they'll be good to help keep you motivated. Could we walk to your house after school?"

Sandy looked away. "No, my mother works at home, and I couldn't interrupt her," she said quickly. "But there's a park near my house—we could meet there."

I shrugged. "OK. I'll walk with you there after school and ask my stepfather to pick me up later."

"I gotta go now," Sandy said abruptly.

She walked away, her tent dress rustling, and I called out after her, "Don't forget to write down everything you eat or drink. And be honest!"

I went to my locker then waited in the hall in case Chip should show up early. He never does. In fact, he usually bursts through the door just as the tardy bell is ringing. Punctuality is not exactly one of his strong points.

But he's got other strong points that I love. He's kind, he loves dogs, and he's never been afraid to try anything new. In eighth grade he tried out for the part of Curly in our school production of *Oklahoma!* and that's where I really got to know him. I sang the part of Laurie opposite him, and from the first time I looked into his blue eyes, I was hooked. We got to be friends, and then we started going to church together. Chip was the one who told me what being a Christian was really all about.

I owe him a lot. When my dad left home, I didn't think anybody could understand the hurt I felt, but Chip was there for me. He has a nearly perfect family, of course, but he helped me see things I hadn't wanted to see.

I hadn't had a chance to explain to Chip why I

was working on Sandy Shore, and I thought he'd be happy about my project. He once told me the Christian life was all about serving God, and I knew that my project with Sandy would please God. It was the nicest—and the toughest—thing I've ever tried to do for someone else. I thought Chip would be excited about it.

It was about three minutes before the bell when I saw Chip coming down the hall. I walked out to meet him, stepping through clusters of kids in the hall. Just then, up ahead, I saw Sandy Shore walking slowly to her first period class. There were two boys behind her, and they were exaggerating Sandy's walk by swaying their hips from side to side. Their laughter rang down the hall.

"It looks like two cats fighting under a sheet," one boy crowed, making no effort to lower his voice.

I stopped in my tracks. I know Sandy heard him. There was no way she couldn't have.

Chip had reached me and saw the shocked look on my face. "What's wrong?" he asked.

"Nothing." I gritted my teeth as the two boys sashayed their way on down the hall behind Sandy. "Nothing that my latest project won't cure."

"Your what?" Chip asked, but I didn't have time to answer. The bell rang, and we had to sprint for our first-period class.

8

I met Sandy after school, and we walked to her neighborhood, a subdivision not more than half a mile from the school. "My house is right down that street," Sandy said, pointing vaguely to a street that veered off to our right. "But here's the park. I love to come here, except, of course, when my favorite programs are on TV."

"What are your favorite programs?" Since she was in such a talkative mood, I thought I'd just let her rattle on for a while. Sandy had never really opened up to me before.

"I love all the shows on WOBG," she said, settling onto a swing.

"The Oldies-but-Goodies channel?" I laughed. I found a swing next to hers.

"Yes. I like 'Leave it to Beaver' and 'My Three Sons' and 'Father Knows Best.'" She ran backward and jumped into her swing then pushed with all her might. Sandy might not think of herself as athletic, but that girl could swing.

"What's your favorite *new* show?" I asked, trying to keep my swing in line with hers. "I don't watch those old ones very much."

She leaned backward so far that her ponytail dragged in the dirt as the swing passed me. "I really only like 'The Cosby Show.' None of those others are very good. All the families in the other shows are all messed up. There's a mother gone, or a father who's an alien, or three fathers and no mother, or two mothers and a butler. I like shows about real life."

I thought about what she said. I had never realized that most of the popular shows on TV had crazy families. But then, I had a crazy family, too—and mine was real life. "Oh, I don't know," I answered finally. "Real life can be pretty weird sometimes." I shrugged. "Shouldn't we get started? You need to give me your food list for today."

"In a minute." She leaned back again, totally relaxed in her swing. As she flew through the air, again and again, I could see why she liked swinging so much. She didn't look heavy. She probably didn't feel heavy, either, flying through the air like that.

"My father had the best surprise for my mother the other day," Sandy said, dreamily. I stopped my swing to listen because there was no way I could keep up. "It was their twentieth anniversary, and Meredith took Mom out for the afternoon so Dad could fix the house up to look like the college cafeteria where he proposed to her. He hired a cook, and a band, and Michael and I fixed the house all up. It was beautiful."

"Wasn't that—" I started to ask, then stopped. I was sure I had just seen that same thing last week on a rerun of "The Cosby Show." But I didn't want to sound like I thought Sandy was lying. Besides, on "The Cosby Show," the father had fixed their house up like a restaurant, not a cafeteria.

"That's nice," I said.

"It was wonderful," Sandy said, still leaning back with her eyes closed. She stopped pumping and just let the swing drift forward and backward. "They ate a delicious dinner, and then we kids gave them presents, and then we all had a family hug." She opened one eye and peeked over at me. "Does your family ever have family hugs?"

The corner of my mouth went down. "No," I muttered. "I can't say that we've ever had family hugs. We're not much of a family."

"Oh." Sandy closed her eyes and put her head back again as her swing slowed to a stop. She sat up then and shook her head. "So, Coach, what do we do now?"

"I need your food list," I told her. "And write on it only what you plan to eat tonight—no more and no less. Max will put it in the computer, and I'll let you know tomorrow where we stand."

"Well, I know I only have 400 calories left to spend," Sandy said, pulling her food list from her notebook. "So I'll probably eat a peanut butter and jelly sandwich on whole wheat bread. Plus two carrots. I think we have carrots in the fridge."

"OK. Here's an article about social eating that you need to read tonight," I told her, pulling an article from Max's file.

"Social eating?" Sandy was puzzled.

"Yeah. It will help you watch what you eat at parties and in restaurants."

"I don't go to parties."

"You will," I told her. "Believe me, you will."

There was a letter waiting for me and Max when I got home. It was postmarked "Houston, TX." I snatched it, ran to my room, and tore it open:

> Dear Gypsy Girl and Boy Genius:
> Houston is an unbelievable city. I always thought I was cosmopolitan, but coming from Canova Cove to Houston is like going from the moon to Mars. Houston is just so much more. Bigger. Broader. And thousands of more people.

My new job is working out well, and I'm living in an apartment for a while until I find a house or something to settle in permanently. When you guys come to visit this summer, maybe you can help me house-hunt.

I hope school is going well for you two. I've told everyone what incredibly talented kids I have. So Max, keep up your research, and Cassie, keep singing. I want you both to make me proud and rich someday. Ha Ha.

Well, give my best to your mom and if you're not too busy, jot me a note. I love you both.

Dad

"What a stupid letter," I said aloud, not caring who heard me. I didn't care about Houston or his dumb job. I wanted to know that Dad missed me, that he was upset at leaving his son and daughter. I wanted to know *why* he didn't even come tell me good-bye before he left. I wanted to know so many things— and Dad spent his entire letter talking about stupid Houston!

I bet he never really told anyone he was proud of his kids, I thought angrily. *I bet he wants to forget he even has kids.* I scrunched up the letter and threw it across the room. I just couldn't understand it. How could

Dad just up and move away like that? He had to care about leaving me and Max—and he had to realize how much we would miss him! Unless . . .

Suddenly I sat up, startled. Dad could never have just moved away like that, unless . . . unless, since we have Tom for a stepfather, Dad figured we don't need him anymore.

That had to be it. I jumped up and went to pick up the crumpled letter. Maybe if I wrote Dad and told him how much I loved and needed him—and how rotten Tom was—maybe Dad would feel better. Maybe he'd even come back. Dad had to know that Tom couldn't replace him. Not ever.

I yelled for Max. "Come here! We have a letter from Dad!"

"Shhhh! Stephanie is asleep," Max warned, but he came out of his room and read the letter with interest. When he was done, he gave it back to me. "That's nice," he said simply and started to walk away.

"Max, sit down a minute," I said, pulling him down on the floor. We sat on the carpet, and I tilted my head so I could see into his eyes. "I think Dad feels that we don't need him anymore because we have Tom. I think maybe Dad left because he felt left out. You know how sensitive he is; he probably wants us to forget all about him and just accept Tom as our father."

Max was skeptical. "I don't think so, Cassie," he said. "Dad has always talked about how neat it would be to work for NASA in Houston. This job was a big promotion for him."

"No, I just know that isn't why he left," I insisted. "Our dad did an incredible thing. He sacrificed his right to see his own kids so that we'd be happy with Tom. Can't you see that? He didn't want us to be torn between two fathers, so he just up and moved away. Max, that took courage! I mean, haven't you wondered how he could leave us? I know he wouldn't do it unless he thought it was the best thing for us. He loves us too much to just move away because of a job!"

Max looked down at the carpet and his chin quivered a little bit. Sometimes I get so carried away with Max's genius that I forget he's only a ten-year-old boy.

"I guess so," he finally said, running his fingers over the carpet. Then he looked up, and his brown eyes were swimming in tears. "So what are we supposed to do about it? We can't do anything."

"Yes, we can. We can write him a letter and let him know that we understand. And we can tell him that moving won't change anything. We still need him, we want him to be our father, and Tom will *never* take his place. We'll say we're miserable, and that Tom isn't like a real father—"

"Tom is really nice," Max interrupted. "You can't say he's done anything wrong."

"I won't say he's done anything wrong," I muttered. "I'll just say he's not a good father. That we can't talk to him. Or that he treats Nick a lot different than he treats us."

Max was doubtful. "I still don't know. Do we have to make Tom look bad?"

"If we want Dad back, we do," I answered. "Don't worry, Max. I'll write the letter tonight. All you have to do is sign it."

I like writing. In fact, I keep a black notebook in which I write poems, songs, and stories that I like. Nobody else is allowed to read my black notebook, not even Mom. Especially not Mom. Her hair would turn gray if she read some of the stuff I wrote!

I flipped through my notebook to see if there was any really gushy stuff I had already written that I could use in my letter. I did find a poem by Emily Dickinson that was great:

> *After great pain a formal feeling comes—*
> *The nerves sit ceremonious like tombs—*

but Dad might recognize the lines and know I'd copied them from a book.

Finally I found a poem I wrote for the Challenger astronauts. Dad had never seen it, and it would work for him, too, with a few changes. So I wrote:

Dearest Dad:
The early twilight settles around the world,
The silvery hush wraps itself around the
    earth.
I sit quietly, missing you.

The afternoon's rain steadily drips from off
    the rooftops.
The buzz of the cricket adds to nature's melody.
But my heart sings only of you.

The gentle breeze brushes my cheek and fingers
    my hair.
The sweetness of day's closing and evening's
    advent calms my soul—
But I feel only the want of you.

There is another in our house, with his own
    son and daughter,
But he is not you, nor is he our father.
He will always be a stranger to us.

I know you have thought to ease our pain,
To give us a new father, with material gain,
But, dearest Dad, we want you.

> Love always,
> Cassie and Max

Max and I signed the letter, and I mailed it the next morning.

9

"Max says you're doing fine," I told Sandy the next morning. "But you need to eat more fiber and less fat and protein. Cut down on the diet colas, too, because they're high in sodium. Drink more water."

Sandy rolled her eyes. "I don't know how to eat more fiber and less fat."

"Max says to read the labels on anything you put in your mouth," I told her. "And stay away from anything fried—that's where the fat is. Snack on fruits and vegetables instead of crackers."

"OK." Sandy looked discouraged, but she stepped onto the scale and didn't hide her eyes like she usually did. She just looked down at the floor, and when the scale finally balanced and I didn't say anything, she looked up in despair. "Don't tell me! I gained again!"

"Nope." I was grinning. "You've lost five pounds in your first week, Sandra Cheryl Shore. Congratulations!"

She stepped back in shock and almost lost her balance. "You're kidding. Really?"

"No, I'm not kidding. You weighed in today at 155."

"That's incredible." A light gleamed in her eyes as her success finally began to dawn on her. "You know, I even feel skinnier."

"You should. Now here's your article for today. Read it when you have a chance. But it would be best to read it at lunch, I think."

Sandy took the article and glanced at it. "What are we studying today?"

"Improving your eating habits by chewing your food well and taking smaller bites," I said, marking Sandy's weight in my notebook. "It's psychological warfare against fat."

"Sounds good." She stuffed the paper in her book bag and started to walk away.

"When you get down to 153, I have a surprise for you," I called after her. "We're going to do your hair and makeup. Soon everyone will wonder who the gorgeous new girl is."

Sandy didn't even turn around, but I didn't care. My project was succeeding wonderfully. All my work would soon pay off, and then everyone would see that I was not self-centered. I do care about other people, and Sandy Shore was going to prove that to the world.

Chip was actually *early* for school, so I led him to

a bench by our lockers. I explained my entire project, and Chip listened without interrupting. "Then I'm going to teach her how to dress, and how to walk, and make her stop biting her nails," I told him. "Then, I'll get her a date for the Spring Fling, too. She'll be an entirely new person, Chip. Won't that be great? No one will pick on her anymore."

Chip shook his head and reached for my hand. "Cassie, why are you doing this?"

I was surprised the answer wasn't obvious. "For Sandy, of course. And for God. Doesn't God like it when we help other people?"

Chip shrugged. "Sure, if we do things unselfishly. But have you stopped to think that maybe Sandy was happy the way she was? What if she doesn't want to turn into a social butterfly?"

I was slightly insulted. "Why wouldn't she want to have fun and look better? Every girl wants to look good, Chip. You guys just don't understand. For some reason, probably because she never outgrew her baby fat, Sandy has been big. Because she's big, people make fun of her. Because people make fun of her, she doesn't want to do anything for herself. But I'm going to teach her to care."

Chip shook his head. "It isn't that easy. You can't remodel people like you would a house."

"Oh, yes you can," I teased him. I wasn't going to

let him discourage me. "You just wait and see. She'll be so pretty when I'm done with her that I just might have to get a tiny bit jealous of Sandy Shore."

It hurt my feelings a little that Chip wasn't more excited about my project. I thought he'd rave about how selfless and nice I was to help our class misfit. Apparently he thought Sandy was a hopeless case. That was surprising, because Chip isn't easily discouraged. He helps his uncle the vet at the animal hospital a lot, and Chip's always telling me about some dog that wasn't going to make it but did after his uncle worked on it all night. Chip has always had room for hope, so why didn't he have any for Sandy?

What would it be like to be Sandy? I wondered. I knew she had a great older sister and an older brother who was a troublemaker, but then again, lots of my friends have trouble-making brothers. She obviously has a nice mother and father. And at least she's never had to deal with divorce. They must have a happy family.

She probably feels secure only at home, I thought, *because there's no way she could feel secure at school.* I was beginning to notice how other people treated her. I'd already seen the boys making fun of her, but I also noticed that teachers talked to her as if she were retarded or just slightly stupid. Whenever she asked a question, which wasn't often, the teachers sighed, looked exasperated, and answered loudly in clear and simple terms. She always sat in the far corner of any room, against the wall, and no one voluntarily sat next to her unless there was nowhere else to sit.

Sandy worked alone in science when everyone else had lab partners. Unless I was with her, watching every mouthful she ate, she ate alone either out under the oak tree or in a back corner of the lunchroom. I could only imagine what gym class was like for her. I knew no one would ever pick her to be on a basketball or softball team, and taking showers in front of the other girls must have been sheer torture.

She had no friends. Her sister was too busy with her activities to bother with Sandy. As for Michael Shore, well, he didn't do much of anything in school but slink around the halls with his buddies decked out in black leather.

No wonder she watched so much TV. At least there she had friends and laughter. And at least she had a mom and a dad who cared about her. They probably hated it that their youngest daughter was a social outcast. But what could they do? If Sandy wanted to ruin her life by eating herself into social ruin, they couldn't stop her. But I could. At least, I could try.

I thought about Sandy's dad fixing up their house for his anniversary. My dad was never really that crazy, but he had been great when he lived with us. I could still see the way his dancing black eyes would snap, and hear him singing to me all the time in his Irish tenor. His voice was just one of his many talents. He was handsome and charming, and nobody on earth could pick a better Italian restaurant.

I sure missed him.

Maybe Sandy Shore didn't have it so bad after all. She had a dad, anyway, who lived at home and loved her enough to have family hugs. I'd give my favorite earrings for a family hug, as long as my dad was in it.

10

Sandy wasn't alone at the gym on Monday morning. Meredith Shore was there, too, waving a piece of paper under Sandy's nose and gesturing dramatically. I had always wanted to meet her, so I hurried over.

"Hi," I said, breathless from hurrying.

Meredith Shore just looked at me the way a lot of seniors look at us underclassmen. "Hi," she answered, without interest. She turned back to Sandy. "Now Sandy, this list is really important, so as soon as you get home, you get started, OK? You know I don't get off work until six tonight, so you've got to get these chores done and dinner started. Just don't turn on the TV until you're through, OK? I'll be home at six-thirty, and then I'll take over."

Man, was Meredith Shore ever bossy! How could Sandy put up with being bossed around like that? But Sandy didn't seem to mind. She took the paper, tossed it into her messy book bag, and sighed. "OK."

"You promise?"

"I promise."

Meredith left us without a backward glance, and when she was gone, I whistled. "Boy, is she always like that? She's like a drill sergeant!"

Sandy shrugged and rubbed her nose awkwardly. "Mom's working late today, and so I have to help out, that's all. It's just for today."

I opened the gym door, and we went in. "So how'd you do this weekend?" I asked. "Did you stick to twelve hundred calories a day? Did you remember to eat lots of celery?"

"I really tried," Sandy said. "I was really good. I didn't eat one bad thing."

She climbed eagerly on the scale, and I fumbled with the weights. "It's been three days since I was last weighed," she said. "I'll bet I've lost two, maybe three pounds."

The scale balanced. "Sorry," I whispered. "You're still at 155. Sometimes your body hits a plateau, you know, and you have to keep being careful while your metabolism catches up."

"I can't believe it!" Sandy was honestly upset. "I didn't cheat once, I promise! I drank enough water to flood the house! I even had to go to the bathroom every thirty minutes!"

I laughed. "It's OK, Sandy, maybe it'll show up tomorrow as a weight loss. Don't worry about it. The important thing is that you're learning to control your weight and watch what you're eating."

I gave her the next article from Max. "Max says this one is good for helping you learn how to make small portions seem larger. Also, Max says to remember that you don't have to clean your plate. Just tell yourself that it's better to *waste* unneeded food than have it go to your *waist.*"

"That'll be hard in my house," Sandy admitted. "I've always been taught to eat everything on my plate because the children in Africa are starving."

"You won't help the starving children by being overweight," I pointed out. "Don't take more food than you can eat. That way you won't waste it. But don't eat heaping amounts just because of habit, either. Those few extra bites add up, you know."

Sandy sighed and took the paper. She was about to toss it into her messy book bag, but I took it from her first. "Before you toss it in there, you need to straighten these things out," I told her. I reached into her bag and took out a handful of scrunched up papers. "My mom says an organized life begins with an organized purse. In your case, I think we should begin with your book bag." I smiled at Sandy, so she wouldn't think I was being too pushy, but she just stood there. *She's probably used to Meredith telling her what to do,* I thought.

I pulled out Meredith's list and looked it over. "At least you'll be getting your exercise," I said, looking at the list. "Vacuum the floors, sweep the porch, feed the dog, change the sheets—that's a lot of work, Sandy."

Sandy took her papers from me and smoothed them. "It's OK," she said. "It's just this once. Some-one's got to do that stuff, right?"

"Sure." I watched Sandy hurriedly stuff the papers back into her bag. Her face was red and her eyes looked all watery—something I said had upset her. I reached out and touched her arm. "Sandy, is it Mere-dith? Does she boss you around like that all the time? Is that why you're upset?"

Sandy yanked her book bag off the floor and stood up. "I'm not upset," she said softly, but every-thing in her face and manner told me she was. "I've got to go now."

Off she went, out the door, alone once again, and I was frustrated. There was no getting inside Sandy Shore. But at least I had an important clue—that girl was harassed by her older, overachieving sister. Maybe that's why Sandy Shore thought it was use-less to compete. Meredith Shore was such an over-achiever, she made Sandy Shore look like a zero in comparison.

Chip and I were in the lunch line when Andrea

walked by with her tray. "Your friend the beached whale is putting on quite a show out there in the lunchroom," Andrea crooned. "And I thought you had her on a diet!"

"What's going on?" I asked, but Andrea just laughed and walked out toward the tables. Chip and I paid for our lunches and walked into the large room where everyone ate.

Sandy was sitting at a table by herself with a lunch tray instead of the lunch I knew she'd brought from home. On her tray were three hamburgers, four baskets of French fries, and three wrappers from extra-large Snickers bars. Even as I watched in horror, Sandy was stuffing the last of a Snickers bar into her mouth.

Worse yet, a group of kids was standing around and watching her eat. "Go, go, go!" they chanted, and with every cheer Sandy stuffed more and more food into her mouth.

She froze for a second when she saw me, but then she licked her chocolate-smeared finger clean and put a two-fisted grip on a cheeseburger.

"I can't look," I whispered to Chip. I turned around and hung my head. "I can't watch. Please. What's happening, Chip? Why is she doing this?"

Chip looked back at Sandy one more time, then

he led me to another table. "Come on, Cass, you don't want to be part of that crowd."

We left for the far corner of the cafeteria, but the cheers and roars continued around Sandy Shore for another five minutes until a teacher arrived and made everyone sit down. My great plan and project was falling down around me, and I didn't have the faintest idea why.

The rest of the day only got worse. On the way home, Tom and Max rattled on about their latest addition to their odd objects collection, some weird plant from Africa that looks like a rock. "It's a Lithops plant," Tom explained. "A stemless plant that camouflages itself."

I didn't say anything. I could only think about the unbelievable sight I'd seen that afternoon: shy Sandy Shore, surrounded by food, and eating like a pig as the rowdiest kids in our school cheered her on.

At home, I walked through the door in a daze and almost didn't hear Tom when he said, "Cassie? Your mom's out shopping, and I've got to have a quick meeting with a client. Keep an ear out for Stephanie, will you? She should be waking up from her nap any time now."

I nodded, then went back to my homework. I still

didn't like being used as a baby-sitter, but Nick and Max were home, too, so it wasn't like I was singled out for the honor. Plus, I was in my room, and Stephanie's nursery was right down the hall.

She did begin to cry about ten minutes later, and I went in and picked her up. She was glad to see me, but her diaper was soaked. I changed her diaper, bundled up the wet disposable and threw it into her special garbage pail. Not knowing what else to do, I took her back to my room and let her crawl around on the carpet while I finished my homework.

She was happily chasing Dribbles's tail when I heard the front door open. Mom was home, and I ran out to the landing to look downstairs to see if maybe she'd bought something for me. I could tell in a quick glance that all her packages were from Baby Boutique. Rats.

When I got back in my room, Stephanie was sitting up, calmly eating my geometry homework. A huge corner of my paper was soaked with baby drool, and another section was missing. Little wadded-up pieces of paper were covered in baby slobber and scattered around the floor.

"You are one spoiled kid," I told her, picking up the disgusting spit wads. "I ought to yell at you for this. If I thought any one of those problems was right, I would. But they're all wrong, so I'll have to do them over again anyway." I scooped her up and put her on my hip. "Come on, let's go see what Mom bought you."

We went downstairs just as Tom came through the door, too. Mom kissed him, then held out her arms for Stephanie. I handed the baby over, then looked around at the packages. "Need some help taking them upstairs?" I asked. Maybe it was time to ask Mom for some advice about Sandy Shore. This would be a good time for us to talk.

"Thanks, Cass," Mom said.

She was pointing out which box I should take when suddenly Tom yelled: "Look at her, Claire! She's choking!"

Stephanie's mouth was open in a soundless cry and her face was blood-red. Her blue eyes were open wide, but no sound was coming out.

"What's she choking on?" Mom shrieked, practically tossing Stephanie in the air. "She hasn't had anything to eat!"

Tom was thumping Stephanie on the back, while Mom tried to turn her upside down to dislodge whatever was in her throat. Finally, as Stephanie began to turn blue, Tom kicked the packages on the floor apart and lay Stephanie on the carpet. He pushed her head back and opened her mouth.

"There's something on the roof of her mouth," he

yelled. He stuck his finger in her mouth and scraped something out—a tattered corner of my geometry paper.

Free of the paper that had blocked her windpipe, Stephanie screamed in earnest while Mom soothed her. Tom just stood there with the paper on his finger. "What in the world?" he asked. "How did she get this?"

"She ate my homework," I said, my legs suddenly feeling weak. "I left her for a minute, and she chewed up my homework."

Tom yelled so loudly that the grandfather clock in the hall chimed. "Cassiopeia Priscilla Perkins!" he roared. "You could have killed this baby!"

"Tom!" Mom snapped. "It's not her fault. It's OK."

"No," Tom lowered his head and glared at me. "You *never* leave a baby alone, do you understand? I left you in charge, and you left her alone, and she could have been killed. Do you understand what you have done?"

I couldn't even answer. I wanted the floor to open up and swallow me whole. I wanted to be thrown into the fireplace or locked for a week in a closet with no food. How could I have been so stupid? But babies are always eating things. How was I supposed to know she had a piece of my paper still in her mouth?

"I—" I tried to answer, but Tom interrupted me.

"You go to your room, young lady," he ordered. "You will not eat dinner with us. You will not go anywhere or do anything except go to school for two months. And you will not be trusted with this baby again."

I turned and ran up the stairs as fast as I could.

11

Grounded for two months! It was incredible. I had turned my back on Stephanie for two minutes— and now I was grounded for two months! Sixty days. One thousand, four hundred and forty hours. Eighty-six thousand, four hundred minutes. Five million, one-hundred-and-eighty-four thousand seconds. Any way I looked at it, it was an unfair sentence.

I knew my dad would never have flown off the handle the way Tom did. Even my mom seemed to understand that babies get into things. I certainly didn't do anything wrong on purpose.

Mom did knock on my door later and tell me to come down for dinner, so I went down to eat with everyone else. But I was quiet. Max tried to lighten the atmosphere by telling us that the new McDonald's lean deluxe hamburger was based on an algae-based food additive, but not even that news made things any better.

Nick was interested, though. "You sold an algae

formula to a company, didn't you? Do you get money from McDonald's, too?" he asked.

"No," Max shook his head. "When I sold my formula to the dog food company, they bought all rights to market the algae additive. I'm just glad to know that people have finally wised up to the advantages of algae."

"That's gross, Max," Mom interrupted. "Let's talk about something else."

Max looked at me, but I stared down at my plate. Jambalaya was one of my favorite dishes, and Uncle Jacob had knocked himself out preparing this one, but I just wasn't in the mood for food.

"The dinner is great, Jacob," Tom said, trying to make conversation.

"I wanted fresh tomatoes," Uncle Jacob grumbled, which was his usual way of handling a compliment. "But I had to use canned. So it's not as fresh as I like it."

"Did you know that it is legally allowable to have two maggots in a seventeen-ounce can of tomatoes?" Max offered helpfully. "The government even allows thirty-five fruit fly eggs per every eight ounces of golden raisins."

"Disgusting." Nick put down his fork and looked at his plate. "Do I have to eat this?"

"You might as well," Max said, taking a huge bite.

"Actually, the more bugs that are in our foods, the fewer pesticides farmers have to use to grow them. When you think about it, it's probably better for you to eat bugs than poisonous chemicals."

"Well, I'm not eating canned tomatoes or raisins," Nick said, pushing his plate away.

"It doesn't matter what you eat," Max said, spooning up another mouthful. "Up to 6 percent of potato chips are allowed to be from rotten potatoes. Chocolate is allowed to contain one rodent hair per one large candy bar. Peaches are allowed to be—"

"Max, that's enough," Mom interrupted. She was picking at her dinner, too, but I don't think it was because of what Max was saying. She seemed to be as bothered as I was about Tom's scene this afternoon.

When we had all finished, Tom cleared his throat. "Cassie, your mother and I would like to see you in the library, please. Boys, you help Uncle Jacob clear the table."

I would rather have dish duty than face Tom again, but I pushed my chair back and stood up. "I'll be in the library," I told him. They were the last words I ever wanted to speak to him.

I sat in the wing chair and waited for them to come in. When they finally did, Tom came right to the point. "Cassie, your mother feels I was too harsh by grounding you for two months," he said, standing over me. "So let's make it one month instead."

"Tom, that's not what I meant," Mom interrupted. She sat back on the couch and smiled at me. "It was an accident, and Cassie has learned her lesson. It could have happened to any of us, even me or you. Cassie, you're not grounded at all. Just remember to be careful when you're watching the baby."

Tom turned slowly and looked at Mom. For a minute he stuttered without words, then his hand went to his forehead. I could tell he wanted to yell, but his lips flattened out as he clenched his teeth together. "How can I be the head of this family if you won't let me discipline the children as I see fit?" he said, his face turning a bright red.

He took a deep breath and the words poured out: "You told me, Claire, that you wanted me to treat your children as if they were my own. Well, Cassie was so concerned about herself that she forgot to look after the baby. I'd ground Nick for pulling a crazy stunt like that. Yet here you are trying to overrule me because it concerns Cassie."

"I'm not overruling you because it's Cassie," Mom answered, her eyes filling with tears. "I just think it's an unjust punishment, that's all. If it had happened to Nick, I wouldn't want him grounded, either."

"But you wouldn't interfere."

Tom's words hung in the air, and we all knew they were true. Mom did treat Max and me differently than she treated Nick. She wasn't mean to him or anything, it was just that she didn't really *mother* him the way she was always looking after us.

Mom kept her head up, but she looked away. I could tell she felt confused and guilty. I felt myself getting angry. Mom was right! How dare Tom make her feel this way!

Before I knew what I was doing, I jumped up and stood right in front of Tom. "I hate you," I said slowly and evenly. "I hate you, I hate you, I hate you."

I thought Mom would back me up, but I heard her gasp: "Cassie!" I glanced over at her. Mom was as white as a sheet, and her hand covered her mouth as if she'd said it, not me.

It didn't matter. I left them in the library and ran upstairs to my room. Soon my dad would get my letter and realize he didn't have to run away from us. He would know that we needed him, and he'd come home. Soon my dad would be back with us, and Tom could go to China, for all I cared. He could even take Nick and his Tibetan nose-pickers with him.

A quiet little voice inside me reminded me that Max would honestly hate to see Tom go. And Stephanie—well, Stephanie belonged to Mom, me, and Max, didn't she? She'd been carried in my mom's belly, and she was ours.

So I told that little voice to shut up. I lay on my bed and when Dribbles tried to jump in bed with me, I turned my back and ignored him. Tom Harris gave me that dog, so when the time came to leave Tom Harris, Dribbles could just stay. If Tom Harris didn't want a self-centered stepdaughter, he didn't have to have one.

After Friday's scene in the cafeteria, I was a little surprised that Sandy Shore showed up at the gym on Monday morning. "I'm sorry," she said simply as we walked to the scales. "I guess I just had a setback, that's all. I'd been craving so many foods that I just couldn't help myself."

"That's OK," I told her firmly. "Let's see how you did over the weekend."

I couldn't believe it, but Sandy had actually lost two more pounds. "You did great!" I congratulated her. "What did you do to yourself? You're down to 153!"

Sandy grinned at me. "I walked around the block every morning and every night," she said. "It looked easy, and it was even fun. I think I'm going to do it as often as I can."

"That's great." I tried to be encouraging. I certainly didn't want to get her upset and have a repeat of Friday's performance. "Say, Sandra," I said, placing an emphasis on her new name, "why don't you eat lunch with me today in the cafeteria? You don't have to eat outside, you know. If you want to make friends, you need to go where the people are."

"I don't know." I knew Sandy was embarrassed about last Friday.

"Listen, my dad says if you fall off a horse, you've got to get back up and ride again right away. You fell off your food plan, that's all. Now you've got to go back in there and face that crowd. You'll see, it'll be easier than you think."

Sandy was still doubtful. "You'll be with me?"

"I promise. I'll meet you at the cafeteria door, and we'll go in together and eat lunch. No one will say a thing, you just wait and see."

Sandy nodded slowly, and I breathed a sigh of relief. Great. If I could get her to make some new friends, then she'd be well on her way. My project would be successful, and Mom and Tom and everyone would know that I was *not* totally concerned about myself. Tom would see that I was basically a nice, caring person, and that whole thing with Stephanie had been an accident. Best of all, just as soon as Tom learned to appreciate me, my dad would come back and take me away from Tom Harris. Good riddance.

I was on my way to the lunchroom to meet Sandy when I nearly ran into Andrea and Blakely Russo in the hall. Andrea's books were on the floor, and she stood in the hall with her hands clenched into fists. Blakely's china-blue eyes were wide open in surprise.

"Don't you lie to me, Blakely," Andrea snarled. "I know you're out to get Eric from me. I saw you talking to him after second period."

Blakely was calm. "Is there a law against talking to someone?" she asked, batting her eyes. "Honestly, Andrea, I'm not trying to take your boyfriend. What would I want with him?"

"You take that back!" Andrea yelled.

Blakely laughed. "Take what back? That I don't want your boyfriend? Honestly, girl, you're out of your mind."

Andrea's hand swung back, and I caught it before she had a chance to slap Blakely. "Forget it, Andrea," I said, holding her arm tightly. "She doesn't want your boyfriend. Eric wouldn't want to go out with her anyway."

Andrea seemed to calm down a little bit, and Blakely turned and walked away from us. "There, she's leaving," I said. "Can I let go of you now? You promise you won't run after her and get into a fight?"

"I hate that girl," Andrea fumed, glaring at Blakely's retreating head. "She thinks she can have any guy, any time. She drives me absolutely crazy!"

"She drives everyone crazy," I said, letting go of Andrea's arm. I stooped to help her pick up her books. "Come on, you're going to miss lunch if you don't hurry."

Andrea bent down and reached for her books, too, jabbering all the while about how Blakely was flirting with Eric, and while Eric and Andrea were still going strong, it didn't help to know that Eric thought Blakely was pretty, and Andrea just couldn't help feeling out of it. . . .

I listened to her babble for about ten minutes, then I remembered I was supposed to meet Sandy at the cafeteria. "I have to go," I told Andrea. "Stay calm. Go eat lunch with Eric. You'll feel better."

"Where are you going?" Andrea looked up at me as if seeing me for the first time.

"I'm eating lunch with Sandy Shore," I called over my shoulder as I took off. "You wouldn't believe how well she's doing."

12

Sandy wasn't waiting by the door. I ran outside and looked for her on the lawn, but she wasn't there, either. I peeked into the library, another of Sandy's favorite hiding places, but she wasn't there. Finally I went through the lunch line and saw Sandy sitting alone in the cafeteria.

She was nearly done with her salad when I reached her. "I'm so sorry," I apologized as I sat down. "I stopped to break up a fight between Andrea Milford and Blakely Russo, then Andrea had to tell me all about it." I opened my milk carton and stuck in a straw. "Actually, that was the first time Andrea's really talked to me all year. I just couldn't walk off and leave her."

"It's OK, it's my fault," Sandy moaned. She leaned her head on her hand and looked as gloomy as a kid who's slept through Christmas. "I should have known this wasn't a good idea. I just don't belong here, Cassie."

"Why not?" I looked around. Everyone was going

about their business in the usual way, and as far as I could tell, no one had bothered Sandy.

"If you hadn't promised to meet me, you could have stayed and talked to Andrea longer. You and Andrea would probably be best friends if you didn't have to spend so much time with me. I'm sorry, Cassie. It's all my fault, and I wouldn't blame you for hating me."

I looked at Sandy with my mouth open. "It's not your fault," I said, finally. "Sometimes things just happen. And I'm spending time with you because I want to. And Andrea's not my best friend because she spends all her time with Eric these days."

Sandy just sat there, alone and unhappy. She watched me eat for a few minutes, then deliberately turned her face away and looked out across the cafeteria. I guess watching me eat pepperoni pizza didn't help her much—all she'd had to eat was a cold salad.

I stuffed the last of the pizza into my mouth. "Hey, listen, why don't we get together after school? We can study together or something, plus, I want to do your hair and makeup, remember?"

Sandy stared at me. "Get together?"

"Yeah. I'd invite you to my house except that— well, my stepfather's there and I'm mad at him. You don't know how lucky you are, Sandy, not to have a stepfather."

Sandy nodded. "I guess so."

"Anyway, why don't I come over to your house after school? I could walk with you, we could do our homework, and try out some ideas for a new hairdo. We could do your makeup—do you think your sister would let you borrow some of her stuff?"

"N-no," Sandy stuttered. "I mean, Meredith would say it's OK, but no, you can't come over today. Mom works at home, you know, calling people. She wouldn't want me bringing company over. It distracts her."

"Oh." I picked up a greasy french fry and absently dabbled it in catsup. "Well, would tomorrow be better? Or another day this week?"

"No." Sandy stood up with her tray and bumped her chair under the table with her hip. "I don't think this week is good at all. I'll let you know, OK? I've gotta run now, so I'll see you later."

She was gone, just like that, and I finished my lunch alone. I was surprised how long the lunch period could seem. When you eat lunch with your friends, lunchtime always seems too short. I'd never realized how lonely lunchtime could be. I could see Chip, Andrea, and Eric at our usual table, and I felt like everyone in the school was looking at me, alone at a grungy lunch table and surrounded by empty chairs. How did Sandy Shore stand it?

I didn't mention going over to Sandy's house again. She was doing well on her diet, and maybe she thought having a new haircut and makeup was just too much too soon. So I didn't push her all week, but on Saturday morning I scribbled down Sandy's address from the telephone book, got on my bike, and went to her house. Sometimes you've just got to push people if they're going to get anywhere.

Sandy lived on a street of small houses, some of which were neatly painted and nicely kept. Some of the other houses were in need of repair, and I was a little surprised to find that Sandy lived in one of the saddest little houses on the street. It was a white house, with faded pink trim, and a front yard of black, sandy dirt. I could see a few brave bits of grass trying their best to grow.

As I got closer to Sandy's house, I saw a group of guys on the front porch. I almost kept riding right past the house. Michael Shore was sprawled out in a battered lawn chair. Four of his black-leather buddies were with him. They were smoking, carelessly flicking cigarette ashes into the dirt. Their faces were totally blank. I couldn't tell if they were sad, mad, glad, or just trying to look bad.

I took a deep breath and pedaled my bike up the grease-stained driveway. "Hi, is Sandy home?" I asked.

Michael Shore raised his chin and looked at me. "Who wants to know?" he asked.

"Me," I answered, feeling the hair on my neck rise. "Cassie Perkins."

"She's inside," he said, lazily catching the screen door handle with his hand. He swung the door open and propped it with his boot. "Go on in."

I put down my bike's kickstand and left it in the driveway. I had to walk in front of those four guys, and I felt their eyes burning into me, but I didn't look back. I just kept my eyes on the doorway and went through it.

"Sandy?" I called. Someone was pushing a vacuum cleaner, and all I could hear was its muffled roar. "Sandy?" I peered around a corner into the living room and saw Sandy vacuuming. When she turned off the machine, I called again: "Sandy? Your brother said I could come in."

She whirled around in surprise and gave me a quick smile. "Cassie! Hi. How'd you ever find the place?"

"Max has a map."

"Sandy!" I recognized Meredith's voice. "When you're finished with the carpets, I could use a hand with the laundry!" Meredith came in from the garage, and her hair was sweaty and pulled back with a headband. She was carrying two baskets loaded with laundry, and she gave me a quick glance. "Hi. Nice of you to come, but Sandy's got work to do."

"That's OK. I can help," I volunteered.

Sandy shook her head, but Meredith nodded. "OK. You can both fold clothes, and then—" She pushed a string of damp hair from her forehead. "As soon as I'm done cleaning the garage, I'll make us some lemonade. OK?" She flashed a quick smile and left the room.

Sandy quietly wrapped the vacuum cleaner cord around the machine, and I laughed and pulled a basket of laundry toward the couch. "Boy, is your sister a cleaning fanatic or what?" I asked. "Every time I see her, she's telling you to do something."

Sandy shrugged and pushed the vacuum cleaner into a hall closet. "I guess I'm used to it. But I bet you don't ever have to do anything, do you?"

I laughed again. "We have chores, too, just not as many, I guess. Uncle Jacob runs the house and does the cooking. But Nick, Max, and I have to help with the dishes and stuff. Plus, I have to keep my room clean and baby-sit my sister sometimes."

I bit my lip. I didn't want to talk about the last time I baby-sat Stephanie.

"Well, since Mom works so much and Dad travels a lot, we all help out," Sandy explained. "Even

Michael. He doesn't like to admit it, but Meredith gets after him enough that he'll mow the lawn sometimes—not that there's that much lawn to mow." She sighed. "He may look it, but he's not totally worthless."

She sat down next to me, and we each began pulling clothes out of the laundry baskets. "Make four piles," she said simply. "For Mom, Meredith, me, and Michael. If you don't want to handle anybody's underwear, just throw them over here."

"It's OK." I laughed. "I change diapers sometimes, so handling clean underwear is no big deal."

I noticed Sandy didn't mention her dad. "What about your dad?" I asked. "Doesn't he get a laundry pile?"

"Uh, no, he's been away for a few days," Sandy said, rubbing her nose absently. "So I know none of his clothes were in the wash."

The house was quiet as we worked. No television, no radio, no noise except a low murmur from Michael and his friends as they talked on the porch. "Sure is quiet," I volunteered.

"Mom's asleep," Sandy said. "She worked all night."

"She made calls on a Friday night?" I said, pulling out mismatched socks. "Doesn't seem like many people would be home on a Friday night."

"Oh, yes," Sandy said. "That's one of her best nights. She calls all night, even to California and places in different time zones, so it keeps her up late."

"Oh." I nodded. "I guess we should whisper."

"Not really." Sandy's face broke into a wry smile. "She's sort of a heavy sleeper."

Sandy wasn't exactly a brilliant conversationalist, so I looked around to find something to talk about. Over the big TV in the corner was an old family picture, probably taken when Sandy, Michael, and Meredith were really small. The room was clean, probably thanks to Meredith, but there weren't any little knickknacks. My mother has a thing for collecting little pictures, ceramics, and statues, but Sandy's house was absolutely bare. A couch, a chair, a television, and an old coffee table that spilled old magazines from its lower shelf were alone in Sandy's living room. But people have different tastes. Sandy's mother must like things plain and simple.

We heard Meredith's voice coming through the screen door. "Michael, I told you to start painting the trim an hour ago! The paint is right there next to you, and still you sit here with your do-nothing friends!"

"I ain't painting with pink paint," Michael said slowly.

"You are painting with pink paint, because that's the color of the trim," Meredith answered. "Now you guys get off this porch and get busy or don't expect supper from me tonight! I'm not feeding you unless you get to work!"

The guys grumbled then, but I could hear the scrape of the lawn chairs being pushed back. Meredith obviously had a gift for getting what she wanted.

"And I expect it to look *good*," Meredith called to the guys from the doorway. She let the screen door slam and came in to look at us. "Honestly. What you have to do just to get people to do a little painting."

Meredith went into the kitchen to make lemonade, and Sandy giggled.

13

Sandy seemed to relax after we finished folding the laundry. We sipped lemonade on the couch, and Sandy was quick to point out that it was made with NutraSweet: "Only four calories."

I pointed to the family portrait above the TV and laughed. "That looks about as funny as the one we had done several years ago," I said. "Max and I looked hysterical when we were little."

Sandy smiled up at the picture, too. "I've always liked that picture," she said softly.

"I wish we could take another one, but we can't," I said, putting my lemonade down on the coffee table. "My dad moved out a couple of years ago. Then, last month, he moved away to Texas. I may not see him again until this summer."

Sandy looked down at her lemonade. "At least you'll get to see your dad," she whispered. "I told you something that wasn't exactly true." Her face was pale, and her eyes glittered with held-back tears. "My dad's gone, too. He left us a few years ago, and it's been just Mom, Meredith, Michael, and me. He is a salesman, I think, but I haven't seen him since I was little."

I couldn't believe it. "You lied?" I remembered how wonderful she had made her family sound. "You mean you never see your dad? He didn't really fix up the house for your parents' anniversary? You don't really have family hugs?"

Sandy choked out a noise—a laugh and a sob mingled together. "No. I made that stuff up from something I saw on television. I guess that's why I like TV so much. I see those families and try to imagine what it would be like—"

"You should be used to having one parent by now," I interrupted. I couldn't understand why Sandy acted so weird all the time. "Lots of kids have parents who split up. Mine split up, and I don't sit around fantasizing about TV people."

"You don't ever think about what it would be like if—"

"If my dad came home?" I paused. Yes, I did think about it a lot. In fact, I was really pretty certain my dad would come home as soon as he got my letter. In fact, I was sure he'd received my letter, but he still had details to work out. He had to quit his job, empty his apartment, make plans to move back. . . .

"Sure, I think about it," I admitted. "But that's it. I

don't watch reruns and pretend that people on television are my parents. You've got to stop that, Sandy. It's not good for you."

Sandy only stared at the ice floating in her lemonade. "Maybe you're right. But you don't know anything about me."

"Yes I do." I leaned down so she'd have to look at me. "I know *exactly* what you're going through, Sandra Shore, and I know you can make it through this. Your dad has been gone a long time, and you've got to pull yourself together like Meredith. Just get up and change your life. You can do it!"

Sandy was still quiet, and I had the feeling she had said all she wanted to say. I took my glass into the kitchen and put it on the counter. The house was strangely silent. With three kids at home, you would think there would be activity everywhere. But Michael and his friends had disappeared from the porch. The only sound I heard was the vague rhythmic thumping of the washing machine in the garage.

I looked around for a garbage can so I could spit out my gum. It was tasteless now that I'd drowned it in lemonade, and my gums ached from chewing.

I opened the cupboard under the sink—that's where everyone seems to keep their garbage. Sure enough, there was a can inside. "There you are," I muttered under my breath. I reached in and pulled it out, then leaned over to spit my gum in it.

Just then I caught a whiff of something that made my nose wrinkle. "Ugh!" I muttered with a grimace . . . then stared in surprise. There, among the other garbage, were a bunch of liquor bottles that stank to high heaven. I don't know much about booze, but even I knew that someone must have gotten pretty plastered to empty that many bottles.

I was reading the labels on the bottles when someone tapped me on the shoulder.

"Whaddya think you're doin'?" a rough voice demanded. It was Michael Shore. His snapping dark eyes were less than ten inches from mine. I gulped, swallowing my gum, and stuffed the garbage can back under the sink.

"Uh, nothing," I said, backing away.

"Don't you have someplace to go?" He said, his voice tinged with anger. He pushed himself in front of me and, with one quick movement, pulled out the garbage can and pulled out the bag of trash. Glaring at me, he closed the bag up tightly.

"Uh, yes, I think I'll go home," I said, answering his question with a kind of delayed reaction. I turned and hurried out of the kitchen, aware of Michael's angry eyes burning into me the entire time.

I looked into the living room. Sandy was still sitting on the couch, but she had turned on the television and was watching "The Cosby Show."

"I've gotta go, OK?" I said. "I'll see you in school on Monday."

"OK." Sandy didn't even look up, and I let myself out without letting the screen door slam. I didn't want to get blamed for waking up Mrs. Shore.

I slipped quietly into my own house. Uncle Jacob was puttering around in the kitchen, Mom was upstairs, probably taking a nap, and Nick was out by the pool, probably working on his tan.

I needed to talk to Max. I found him out in the backyard, putting finishing touches on some crazy kind of rocket.

"Can you spare a minute?" I asked. "I need to know something about alcohol."

Max looked at me curiously then gently laid his rocket on the grass. "What about it?"

"I think Michael Shore's been drinking," I said, fidgeting a little. "I found empty liquor bottles in the garbage can in the Shores' kitchen. Michael came in, and when he saw that I'd seen the bottles, he almost bit my head off. Then he took the bottles out and dumped them."

Max shrugged. "It's not really unusual, Cass," he

said. "I read about a poll where more than 30 percent of high school seniors said they had tried alcohol by the time they were thirteen. Another survey found that one in twenty seniors drinks every day."

I sat on the grass and hugged my knees. "I guess I shouldn't be surprised that Michael is drinking. I mean, just look at those guys he hangs around with! But what about Sandy? What if he gets drunk and hits her? Or what if he's drinking when he's driving her someplace and kills her in a car crash? Besides, I don't think Sandy's family has much money, so where's Michael getting the money to buy booze?"

Max shook his head. "Some teenagers drink because they think acting like an idiot is the same thing as being cool," he said a little impatiently. "They don't even consider all the damage alcohol can cause. If Michael's drinking, Cassie, there's nothing you can do about it. He has to make his own decisions."

I thought for a minute, then stood up, brushing the grass from my clothes. "Well, I may not be able to stop Michael from drinking, but I can do one thing. I can tell Sandy to stay out of his way."

I turned and headed back into the house. I was going to slip into the library to find something to read, but when I heard Tom's voice, I paused at the door.

"You're my little darling," Tom was saying to Stephanie. He had spread a blanket out on the floor, and Stephanie was sitting up, watching Tom. She was fascinated. What he did, she did. He raised his hand, she raised hers. He laughed, she laughed. He stuck out his tongue, but Stephanie only creased her forehead. She probably hadn't figured out where her tongue was yet.

It was almost spooky, the way she resembled him. I had never noticed it before, but it was obvious Stephanie was Tom's daughter. It was also obvious to me that if Mom and Tom should ever break up, Tom would fight for Stephanie. He loved her. He was her dad, and she would love him the way I loved my dad.

I felt a sudden sick feeling in my stomach. If Dad did come back, and if Mom and Tom did keep on fighting so much they split up, I might never see Stephanie again. Tom was a good lawyer, and he could win anything he wanted. But even though Steffie was a baby, I really loved her. She partly belonged to me, didn't she? She was my sister!

I ducked away from the doorway and bit my lip to keep from crying. If Dad came back for us, how could I trade him for Stephanie? It wasn't fair, but I knew it was a choice that I might have to make.

A gruff voice interrupted my thoughts. "What's

this? Missy, what do you think you're doing, lurking out here in the hall?"

"Sorry, Uncle Jacob." I tried to keep my head down so he wouldn't see that I had been about to cry. "I'll get out of your way."

"You're not in my way, Missy," Uncle Jacob said, playfully grabbing my arm and pulling me into the kitchen. "Come on in and tell Uncle Jake all about it."

The last thing I wanted to do was talk, but you can't say no to Uncle Jacob about anything. So I gulped down my feelings and tried to act as if nothing was wrong. He'd probably think I was having a case of PMS.

"You can't fool me, Missy. I can see you're upset," he said as I settled onto a stool at the kitchen bar. "Want something cool to drink?"

"A Coke float, please. But use frozen yogurt instead of ice cream." I forced a smile. "Girls have to watch their calories, you know."

Uncle Jacob frowned, but he poured a tall glass of Coke and topped it off with my favorite, vanilla frozen yogurt. He handed me the glass, and I knew the questions would come next.

"Problems with that boyfriend of yours?"

"No, Chip's fine."

"Problems with friends?"

"No, not really."

"Problems at school?"

"No."

Uncle Jacob stopped and glared at me. "You're not making this easy for me, you know."

"Sorry." I took a deep breath. How could I explain all this to him? After all, he was Tom's brother-in-law. Uncle Jacob had been part of the Harris family long before I was.

"I just really miss my dad. I wish he'd come back. Plus, I haven't been getting along so well with Tom, if you haven't noticed. Plus, he and Mom have been fighting, too." I stopped and took a sip of the creamy drink. "So things are really in a mess, aren't they?"

Uncle Jacob propped his elbows on the counter and leaned toward me. "Do you know what empathy is?" he asked abruptly.

"Isn't it like sympathy?"

"Sort of. Empathy is putting yourself in the other person's shoes. It's not just feeling sorry for them, it's feeling what they would feel."

I took another sip. "So?"

"So why don't you try thinking about how Tom's feelin' these days? He fell in love with your mother and thought he'd be a good father to you. I remember those days, Missy, even though you may forget.

Your mother was alone and confused, and I think maybe Tom felt a little bit like a knight on a white horse coming to save the damsel in distress. Maybe now he feels more like he ended up in the dragon's cave—and he's getting burned every time he turns around."

I couldn't help it. I snorted. "My mother is not a damsel in distress. We were doing fine without Tom Harris."

"Fine, maybe, but you weren't doing as well as you are now. Admit it, Missy, because it's the truth."

I scowled at him, but deep in my heart I knew he was right. I don't know if Tom has helped me much, but he really did make my mother a lot happier than she had been in those days. Before she married Tom, she worried about getting old, being poor, and being lonely. Tom had changed all that.

"OK, maybe it's true."

"Well, you also need to remember that Tom took Max in on a moment's notice when your dad skipped town."

A roar welled up within me and I screamed, not caring who would hear. I stood up so fast that my stool toppled and crashed onto the kitchen floor. "My dad didn't skip town! How can you say that? He left because he didn't want us to be torn between two fathers! He left because of Tom!"

Uncle Jacob only shook his head. "Missy, your head is full of rosy dreams," he said. "Be honest with yourself, honey. Your father's a good man, but he's not perfect. He has his faults, just like Tom does. But Tom is trying his best to keep this family together."

Angry words choked in my throat and wouldn't come out. I had thought Uncle Jacob was my friend! How wrong could I be? I'd forgotten he was one of "them," one of the Harrises. I should have known he would join the battle against me in a second.

I rushed out of the room, spilling my Coke float as I left. It was a murky mess, just like everything else. I didn't care. Uncle Jacob could clean it up. Everywhere I went these days, I made a mess.

14

At least one part of my life was going well. Sandy Shore was doing something right, because she was slowly and steadily losing weight. The next Monday morning at school she was down to 148 pounds.

"You're doing great!" I congratulated her. "Here's your sheet from Max for today. It's a lesson on how to keep your family and friends from encouraging you to eat too much."

Sandy looked at the page. "No one at my house even cares how much I eat," she said. "Michael doesn't even look up from his plate, and Meredith usually eats with a book in her other hand."

"Doesn't your mom give you that line about 'I worked hard cooking this, so you'd better eat it'?"

Sandy fidgeted and rubbed her nose. "Not really. Mom works through dinnertime, so Meredith and I do a lot of the cooking." She looked away for a second, then went on. "Mom's a great cook, though. I guess you could tell by looking at me."

"You're not fat, Sandy. You're got to stop thinking of yourself as a fat person."

Sandy sighed. "I can't believe I've lost twelve and a half pounds. I still feel pretty much the same."

I thought about that for a minute. Sandy couldn't tell from her clothes that she was losing weight because all she ever wore were those big tent dresses.

"I've got a great idea." I snapped my fingers. "Let's go shopping. We're going to get you a new outfit for the Spring Fling, plus, we're going to get you some pants!"

"Pants?" Sandy crinkled her nose. "I don't like pants. They're uncomfortable."

"They're only uncomfortable if they're too tight," I said, squeezing her arm. "And they won't be too tight now. You'll love them! We can meet tomorrow after school and go shopping."

"I can't."

What was wrong now? Wouldn't bossy Meredith let her get out of her chores? Then it hit me. Sandy probably didn't have money to go out and buy clothes on an impulse.

"Tell you what," I said, smiling and linking my arm in hers. "I want to treat you to a new outfit. You've gone along with me on this project, and you've earned it."

"I don't know." Sandy was still uncertain, but I could see that she was wavering.

"It's settled. I'll have Tom pick us up and drop us at the mall. We'll have a great time. Then you can come to my house for dinner, and we'll do your hair and makeup. No one at school will even know you the next day!"

Sandy rolled her eyes in protest, but I had learned the best way to handle her was to be firm. She'd come, if only because I ordered her to.

I needed money, and I knew Mom would ask a million questions about why I needed it. I didn't want to tell her about my project just yet. That would spoil the surprise of seeing the new, improved Sandra Shore.

So I had to ask Tom. I had never asked him for anything. Fact is, I usually tried to avoid talking to him altogether. I took a deep breath and went into his study where he was reading legal briefs or something.

"Tom, something special has come up at school, and I need some money," I said. "Actually, I need a new outfit."

"Oh?" Tom looked up at me, and I could see he was surprised that I had even come into the room. He put down his papers and tried to act like everything was normal, but I could tell he was pleased. "How much do you need, Cassie?"

"I don't know. How much can I have?"

Tom laughed and reached for his wallet. "You and your mother are a lot alike," he said. "She usually just takes my wallet and cleans it out."

He handed me two crisp twenty-dollar bills. "Will that be enough?"

I held the bills and looked at them skeptically. "It's a really fancy deal," I said, "I need something really nice."

"OK." Tom handed over another twenty dollars. "But that's enough. You two women are going to drive me to the poorhouse."

"Thanks." I turned and left, glad for the money but a little concerned about what he said. Did he really think Mom spent too much money? I doubted Tom Harris was headed for poverty, but maybe he was too much of a tightwad to get used to my mom. She's a decorator, and she's always liked to have pretty things. *I guess that's the price of being a knight on a white horse,* I thought, *and Tom Harris, I hope it's not more than you bargained for.*

We found a darling outfit for Sandy. I'd seen it featured in *Seventeen,* and I knew it would be perfect for the Spring Fling. It was a sleeveless top with a flared skirt that had lace pants peeking out underneath. Sandy took a size 14, but she had come a long way.

"I can't believe this," Sandy said for about the hundredth time as the clerk handed her the box. "I've never had anything like this."

"You look great in it," I assured her. "Trust me."

"I guess I have to," she said, and she flashed one of her rare smiles.

When Sandy stepped into the brick foyer of our house, she gasped. I grinned at her. "I know, I couldn't believe this house either when I first saw it," I said, pushing her forward. "Come on, let's go up to my room."

In the privacy of my room, I began the make-over of Sandy Shore to Sandra Cheryl Shore. While Sandy looked through copies of *Seventeen* and *Teen,* I combed out her freshly shampooed hair.

"I think you need a trim," I said, eyeing the jagged edges of Sandy's dark hair. "When's the last time you had a hair cut?"

"I cut it myself," Sandy said. "Just whenever I feel like it."

"Oh." No wonder her hair was such a mess. "Well," I pulled on the strings of wet hair and tried to think of what my mother's hairdresser would say. "The straight, smooth look is back in style, and I think you've got the hair for it. Why don't we even your hair up at shoulder length and give you some bangs?"

"Bangs?" Sandy looked at her reflection in my mirror. "I've always worn my hair pulled back in a ponytail. I don't even know if my hair will come down on my forehead."

"You'd be surprised," I told her. "Let me try it."

"Whatever you say." Sandy shrugged and went back to her magazines.

Honestly, this girl was a puzzle! Sometimes she could be as stubborn as a dripping faucet that you can't shut off. But other times she was like putty. I shook my head. I had spent more time with her in the last few weeks than I had with anybody, but I still felt like I hardly knew her.

I combed Sandy's hair into a smooth, shoulder-length style, trimmed the ends, and blew it dry. While she read magazines, I filed and painted her nails.

While she was admiring her nails, she stopped suddenly. "I'm hungry," she said. "I hate to admit it, but I am."

"I'll go see if there are some apples in the pantry," I said. "You stay here and don't mess up your nails. The polish is still wet."

When I came back upstairs with the apples and two Diet Cokes, Nick had his head in my bedroom door. He turned and said, "There you are. Dad wants to know if you are staying home tonight. They need someone to sit with Stephanie."

"Can't you do it?"

"No."

I shrugged. I was a little surprised Tom would let me baby-sit Stephanie after my last disastrous time, but Mom had probably talked him into it. "I'll do it."

Nick went downstairs, idly humming, and I went into my room and gave an apple and a drink to Sandy. Her eyes were wide and her cheeks red.

"Who was that?" she asked in a strangled voice.

"Him? That's just Nick. He's my stepbrother."

Sandy didn't say anything. She just closed her eyes and shook her head slightly. Finally she whispered, "He is wonderful."

I looked back out the door. "Sometimes. Sometimes he's a real pain."

I picked up my makeup brush to finish Sandy's make-over, and an idea hit me. Why not ask Nick to take Sandy to the Spring Fling? Sandy liked him, that much was obvious. And Max was too young to take her, and unless I wanted to let Chip take her, who else would I get to do it?

"How would you like Nick to take you to the Spring Fling?"

Sandy covered her mouth with her hand and

shook her head. "I'd die," she said. "I wouldn't be able to say a word all night."

"He's just a normal guy," I said, brushing blush along Sandy's cheekbone. "See how I'm doing this? You follow your cheekbone up to the hairline and gradually brush it in. Make sure you don't have two red circles on your cheeks."

"He's not 'normal,' Cassie. He's a dream."

"He's OK. Now on special occasions you really should use a lipliner to match your lipstick. It helps your lipstick stay on longer. And you can adjust it so that if your lips aren't full enough, just draw the lines more along the edges of your lips."

I don't know why I bothered to explain my makeup tips because Sandy was obviously in another world. "Then you put mascara on your eyebrows and curl your nose hairs," I went on. "Did you get that?"

"Huh?"

"You haven't heard a word I've said." I stood back and looked at my creation. Sandy Shore really did look like a different person. Her hair now fell softly to her shoulders, with a soft wave. Her face, more slender than I'd ever seen it, showed high cheekbones. And her eyes were large and shining—especially now that she was thinking of Nick.

"You're ready to come downstairs and meet the

family." I snapped my makeup kit shut. "If you want me to fix you up with Nick, you've at least got to meet him officially."

"I can't."

"You've got to."

So Sandy and I went downstairs, and I introduced her to Tom, Mom, Uncle Jacob, and Nick. As Mom asked Sandy polite questions, Max came to stand by me.

"Your project's looking pretty good, Cassie. Is this a test or something?"

"Sort of. I want to get Nick to take her to the Spring Fling."

Max rolled his eyes. "Fat chance. You know he only dates girls from his school."

"That's why I need your help, Max. Help me find some way to beat Nick at something, so he'll have to help me."

"You want to trick him? That's not fair, Cass."

"Come on, you're involved in this project, too! It's for Sandy, and it won't hurt Nick to do something nice for someone."

Max thought a moment. "OK. I'll let you know what I come up with."

15

It was later that night before Max put his plan into action. We were in the den watching television— Max, Nick, and I—and as usual, Nick was flicking the channels to ESPN during all the commercials. I was ready to strangle him because I *like* commercials, but I had to be nice or he'd never help me out.

"You really like sports, don't you?" Max asked, looking up at Nick.

"Yeah." Nick grunted because one of his favorite teams was losing, then flicked the television remote back to the show we had been watching.

"You know a lot about sports, don't you?" Max asked.

Nick looked pleased. "I guess so. I've played about everything."

"Care to have a little contest?"

"What kind of contest? What do I have to do?"

Max sat up straight. "A sports contest. If you lose, you have to do Cassie a favor."

"What favor?"

"Well . . . " Max looked over at me. "Cassie wanted me to trick you, but I decided to make this fair. Cassie, I couldn't trick Nick, but I can give you both an equal chance at winning."

"Max!" I couldn't believe Max was turning traitor.

"It's like this. Nick, if you win the contest, Cassie will do something for you. But if you lose, you have to do something for Cassie. And no matter if you win or lose, you have to take me to a baseball game next week, and Cassie, you have to make my bed for a week." Max grinned. "That's my fee for arranging this little game."

I sighed, but Nick looked interested. "If I win, Cassie has to do something for me?" He grinned at me with a wicked gleam in his eye. "But what's the favor Cassie wants me to do?"

My loving brother Max had turned into a sneak. No matter what happened, I'd be doing his chores for a week. But if Nick agreed to take Sandy to the Spring Fling, it would be worth it.

"OK, Max. I'll make your bed if Nick agrees to take Sandy Shore to the Spring Fling at our school next week."

Nick crinkled his forehead. "Who's that? That girl you had over here earlier?"

I nodded. Nick thought it over, then announced,

"But if I win, Cassie, you have to promise me something."

I sighed. I'd probably have to do his chores for a month. "What?"

Nick's voice was quiet. "You have to promise to go out of your way to be nice to my dad for six months."

It wasn't what I was expecting. Were my feelings about Tom that obvious? Did it upset Nick that I didn't like having his father as my stepfather?

I raised my chin defiantly. "I try to be nice to him. I do."

Nick shook his head. "No, you don't. You have to promise that you'll smile at him, talk to him, and not break any of his rules." He grinned wickedly. "Plus, you have to take him his coffee every morning."

The thought of carrying coffee to Tom Harris first thing every morning was enough to make me sick. There was no way I could do it. But if super-brain Max designed a hard enough contest, there was no way Nick could win.

"I agree."

"OK." Max picked up a notebook. "Nick, I'm going to read three paragraphs about sports. You must tell me if the stories I read are true or false. You must get all three answers correct to win."

"How about best two out of three?"

Max shook his head. "No. You must be precisely right."

Nick thought for a moment, then agreed. "OK. I'm ready."

Max looked at his list. "Number one: Before 1850, golf balls were made of leather and were stuffed with feathers."

Nick thought a minute while I laughed inwardly. Max had really outdone himself on this one! Imagine golf balls stuffed with feathers! Hopefully, Nick would say it was true. It obviously wasn't, and I'd win on the first question!

"True." Nick was firm.

"That's right."

Max consulted his paper again, but I interrupted. "Are you sure? Leather and feathers?"

"It's true, Cass," Max explained. "Trust me." He went on. "Number two: There are bullfights in Detroit twelve times a year."

I laughed out loud. It seemed so easy! Of course there were no bullfights in the United States! The ASPCA and the Humane Society would have a fit if anyone had a bullfight in this country. But Nick would think it was too obviously false, so he'd say true, and he'd be wrong.

"True."

"That's right again." Max looked up at Nick, and they smiled at each other. Was this some sort of male conspiracy?

I couldn't stand it. "How can there be bullfights in this country?"

"Bullfights are not illegal, the matador is just not allowed to kill the bull," Max explained. "They have bullfights in Cobo Arena in Detroit twelve times a year."

I sat back and shut my mouth. How did Nick know so much?

"Number three," Max went on. "In one football season, 18 men were killed in college games and 159 were permanently injured."

"During the game?" Nick asked. "Not in a plane crash or something?"

"During the game," Max said. "True or false?"

Nick thought a moment, and I closed my eyes to concentrate. *Please, please, please miss this one,* I thought hard. I even prayed: *Dear God, would it hurt anything if Nick took Sandy to the Spring Fling?*

"False," Nick said.

Max looked up at me. "It was true," he said. "In 1905, before players wore full equipment, kicking, punching, and gouging were allowed. Eighteen college players were killed."

"That's terrible," I said, feeling sorry for the

players, but it was hard to contain my excitement. Nick lost! He had to take Sandy Shore to the Spring Fling!

Nick sank back in his chair. He looked utterly defeated. "So what do I have to do?" he muttered. "When is this Fling thing?"

I actually could have hugged him. "It's in two weeks. I'll tell Sandy you'll take her, so you don't have to call or anything if you don't want to. And you can go with me and Chip, so you won't be stuck. And Sandy really likes you, you know, so it'll be fine."

He nodded. I couldn't believe he was taking it so well. He really wasn't so bad, at least, not *all* the time.

"And Nick, I'm going to think about what you said. I'll try to be nicer to your dad, I promise. And Max, I'll be glad to make your bed for you. I'll start tomorrow."

I danced out of the room to call Sandy and give her the good news. She'd probably faint, but boy, what an impression she'd make when she entered our school gym in her new outfit with her new face and with my handsome brother on her arm. Even Andrea would be impressed, and all those kids who had made fun of Sandy Shore would be amazed.

Mom and Tom should be there, I said to myself. *That*

would be the perfect time to tell them about my project.
Then they'll see that I'm not self-centered. They'll know
that I'm not thoughtless and stupid and that I can do
something right.

I could ask them to volunteer as chaperons for the
night. Our teachers were always telling us that parent volunteers were needed, and this would be the
perfect night to have Mom and Tom at school.

Maybe things would work out after all.

16

I was almost afraid to open my letter from Dad
when it finally came. Usually if we got a letter at all
it was addressed to Max and me, but this one was
just for "Cassiopeia Perkins," and I knew it was the
answer I'd been waiting for.

I took it to my room and looked at it carefully.
Dad had mailed it four days ago, which means he
had probably been thinking about how to answer
my letter for some time.

"Well," I told myself, "here's your answer, Cassie.
Open it."

I opened the letter and read:

> Dear Cassie:
> Thank you for the lovely poem. I know you wrote
> it, even though Max signed his name, because I
> can recognize your special talents. It's nice to
> know that I am missed because I miss you, too.
>
> I don't know how you feel about your step-
> father, but I want you to know that I don't dis-

like him. As long as he treats you with respect and care, I'm glad that he is there for you because I am not. Nor will I be, Cassie, because I have a new life in Houston now.

We will have great times when you visit in the summer and at Christmas, and we will always have precious memories that no one can take from us. But, Gypsy Girl, the life we once knew is no more, and although it may be hard for you to understand, it can't be that way again.

I'm dating a nice woman out here that you'd like very much. She has kids, too—in fact, there's a girl about your age who reminds me of you. But no one can take your place, Cassiopeia. Remember that.

Give Max a hug for me and keep singing. Send me a tape sometime, OK? I like to brag on my Gypsy Girl.

Love always,
Dad

So. That was that. Dad wasn't coming home. He hadn't left because he wanted to make things easier for me and Max; he left because he wanted a new life with a new woman and new kids. A girl who reminds him of me. *Soon he will forget all about me,* I thought. *If I sent him a tape, he'd only forget about it.*

I sat on the edge of my bed and felt something shrinking inside me. It was like I'd blown Dad up into a larger-than-life parade balloon, and this letter was a sharp pin. I lay my head on my pillow as the life slowly hissed out of my overinflated image of Dad. What was it Uncle Jacob had said—was it all a rosy dream?

I lay there for quite a while. I was too empty to cry. My dad had a new life, and I wasn't even a part of it. Instead of my dad, I had Tom Harris.

Voices from downstairs drifted up to me. Mom was chattering in the kitchen, and Stephanie kept bursting out with baby giggles. Max was explaining something to Nick in a monotone, and Uncle Jacob and Tom were teasing each other about something in the kitchen—not enough, no, too many spices in the crawfish stew.

After a few minutes of listening, I sat up. I didn't just have Tom Harris. I had Mom, Max, Stephanie, Nick, and Uncle Jake. They were my family. Sandy Shore might watch the Huxtables on television and fantasize about a pretend family, but I had more family life downstairs in the kitchen than the Huxtables had in a month of reruns.

Dribbles was lying in his usual place at the foot of my bed, and he raised his head when I slid off the bed. "Come on, Dribs, let's go be sociable," I told him. I folded Dad's letter and put it in my private notebook. Maybe I'd read it again in a few weeks or whenever I needed to remind myself of who my father was. If I felt myself drifting again into a rosy dream, I'd pull out that letter and face reality. But it would always hurt.

Dribs and I went downstairs to join the confusion in the kitchen.

There was an undercurrent of excitement in home-room on Monday. We were nominating girls for Sweetheart of the Spring Fling, and I could see hope in nearly every girl's eyes. Everyone wondered, *Could I be nominated? By some miracle of chances, could I be one of the nominees?*

I wondered myself if maybe Chip or someone would nominate me, but then I decided that no one in their right mind would even think of me. Lately I'd been too busy with Sandy Shore to do much socializing, and it was always the popular girls who were nominated.

There was no hope in Sandy's eyes, either. I looked over at her and was surprised to see how good she looked. She was wearing one of her tent dresses, but her hair was combed out and looked nice. She was wearing a hint of mascara, and her cheeks looked rosy. It wasn't very noticeable that she had lost weight because her dress was so loose, but her face had lost its plumpness and looked pretty. But still, hardly anyone even glanced in her direction.

While we filled out our ballots, I heard Eric Brandt laugh aloud, and a couple of his friends snickered. They were doing something funny, but I didn't want to know what it was. A couple of other kids laughed, too, then turned to scribble something on their ballot forms.

Who should I nominate? I thought of the girls in our class: Blakely Russo, who was stunningly beautiful and would probably get votes from all the guys. Then there was Andrea, who was popular, and Christine Miller, who was sweet, and five or six other girls who were nice. I had a sudden inspiration. "Sandra Cheryl Shore," I wrote on my nomination form. I folded my paper twice and passed it forward.

The five nominees who got the most votes were to be announced that afternoon in a special class assembly. I couldn't imagine who would ultimately win, but at least Sandy Shore had one sincere vote: mine.

17

Miss Boyce, our guidance counselor, stood to make the announcement. "The top five nominees for Spring Fling Sweetheart are Blakely Russo—"

The boys began barking.

"Andrea Milford—"

I could see Andrea blushing. She probably got Eric and all his friends to vote for her.

"Christine Miller—"

Several girls applauded. Christine was well liked and friendly to everyone.

"Cassie Perkins—"

I couldn't believe what I heard. Who had done such a thing? Max? Had Max and his brainy buddies put my name in? Had Chip?

"And Sandy Shore."

A rowdy group of boys began barking again, and Miss Boyce held up her hand for quiet. "You'll have a chance to vote on your choice the morning of the Spring Fling, and we'll announce the winner that night. Until then, we could use volunteers for decorating the gym and selling tickets. If you're interested in being a volunteer, please see me. You're dismissed."

As everyone streamed out of the auditorium, I found Sandy and steered her toward the front where Miss Boyce still stood. "What are we doing?" Sandy protested.

"We're signing you up for the decorating committee and the ticket committee," I said. "The best way to make friends is to get involved, Sandy. And I'm going to get you involved."

The crowd had thinned out, so I dropped her arm and looked at her. There was a flush of excitement on her face, and she really looked pretty. It was too bad no one else had looked at Sandy Shore lately—they were too used to ignoring her. But maybe someone had noticed the changes in her. I suspected that Eric Brandt and his buddies had nominated her for a joke, but just maybe someone had done it because they liked the way she had changed over the last few weeks. I knew I wasn't the only one who voted for her.

"By the way, congratulations on your nomination," I said.

"No. It was a joke, just like the flowers were a joke. But you deserve congratulations, Cassie."

I snorted. "Ha! Just because my brother and his

friends voted for me? Believe me, I'm not taking this seriously."

I walked up to Miss Boyce. "Sandra and I want to volunteer for the decorating committee," I said. "And anything else you need done, we'll be glad to help."

Miss Boyce was young and pretty. "That's wonderful," she said, nodding so enthusiastically that her blonde hair bobbed. "It's not often that our sweetheart nominees volunteer to actually *do* anything."

I shrugged. "We're not much into status, I guess. We just want to help."

Miss Boyce looked over at Sandy, and Sandy blushed and looked down at the ground. "Congratulations, Sandy," Miss Boyce said. "I don't know what you've been doing to yourself, but you seem so much more—well, confident."

It wasn't the right word, but it was nice that she noticed something different. Sandy still wouldn't do anything unless I pushed her into it, but at least I didn't have to push as hard these days.

"The decorating committee will meet today after school to plan and then stay after Thursday afternoon to decorate," Miss Boyce said. "I hope you can both make it."

"We'll be there," I promised. "Come on, Sandra, or we'll be late to class."

Blakely Russo came into English class and put the teacher's wooden bathroom pass on her desk with a clunk. That was no big deal, I mean, everyone has to go through the humiliation of asking for Mrs. Williams's shellacked bathroom pass sometime, but Jaime Stevens muttered something under her breath that I couldn't help overhearing.

"What did you say?" I whispered to Jaime.

"Blakely's been in the bathroom throwing up again," Jaime repeated. "I've seen her do it. After every meal, or anytime she gets nervous, Blakely goes to the bathroom and vomits."

Chip overheard, too. "Gross!"

I couldn't believe it. "Why would she want to do that?"

Jaime jerked her head toward Sandy. "Because she doesn't want to look like el blimpo over there, that's why. How else could she eat like a horse and keep her figure?"

"Shhhh!" I shushed Jaime, hoping Sandy hadn't overheard. Brother! How rude could people be!

But thoughts of Blakely Russo bothered me. How many mornings had Sandy and I seen her slipping into the gym to weigh herself? I thought it was because she was disciplined, not because she was a compulsive vomiter. There was a word for people who did that—bulimic. Was it possible that Blakely,

than I had ever seen her. She pulled a folder out of her notebook. "Last night I did some sketches of decorations for Miss Boyce," she said, opening the folder. Inside were some of the prettiest designs I had ever seen.

"Why, Sandy, you're an artist," I gasped. "I never dreamed!"

Sandy blushed. "I like to doodle," she said simply. "I just never showed anything to anyone before. But I've got to run, Cassie. I promised I'd take these to Miss Boyce before school starts."

For the first time, Sandy went out of the gym before I did. Now she was the leader, and I was following. But I was glad. My experiment was even more successful than I'd ever dreamed it would be. Friday night I would tell Mom and Tom about it, and they'd be impressed. I'd let Max explain what a total misfit Sandy Shore had been, then I'd introduce the new Sandra Shore to them and they'd be floored. I would never, ever, have to hear that I was self-centered again.

Even God had to be pleased.

In second period I was pecking away at my typewriter when suddenly the fire alarm rang. "That's funny," Ms. Templeton said, looking up from her book. "We weren't supposed to have a fire drill today."

We gathered our books, and she stepped out into the hall, but she spun back into the classroom. "Everybody out! Go out the east hall, not the west hall. There's a fire, class, so move out!"

The resulting scene was pandemonium. All one thousand students at Astronaut High School streamed out of the halls, down the stairs, and onto the lawns and parking lots. Thick, black smoke rolled down one hall and lifted lazily toward the sky.

Within five minutes there were three fire trucks on the scene, and they drove right over the lawns and through the rows of buildings. The firemen were deadly serious, and they maneuvered their thick hoses around and we could hear the rush of water from where we stood. The police arrived next. They ran into the building and were questioning our principal and several teachers.

After the initial excitement wore off, we sat down in the grass. Sandy wandered over and carefully placed her books in the grass so she could sit on them and not stain her skirt—a new skirt, and a pretty one.

Max came over, too. "What's up, Max?" I asked.

"Someone was probably smoking in the restroom," Max said, his brown eyes surveying the scene. "I know it wasn't anything in the science labs. I don't think it was anything in the shop, either."

Chip came over and plopped down in the grass. Apparently he didn't care about his clothes or books or hair, because he stretched out in the grass and let the sun shine on his face. "What a way to spend the morning," he yawned. "Is it lunchtime yet?"

"No," Sandy answered. "It's only eleven o'clock." She was watching the scene at school with so much interest she probably forgot about being shy around guys.

I was relieved. If she could talk to Chip, she could talk to Nick. She wouldn't be a bump on a log Friday night. She'd be fine, and Nick wouldn't hate me for making him ask her out.

Nick said Sandy had been polite when he called her. He had reminded her that he was my stepbrother, and then he politely asked her to the Spring Fling. She said, "Yes, thank you, I'd like to go," and Nick told her we'd pick her up. Smooth as silk, Nick said.

"Uh oh," Max said, pointing over at the principal's office. "Something's happening."

Sure enough, two burly policemen came through the door with a sooty teenager handcuffed between them. The boy had his head down, but just before he got into the back of the police car, he lifted his head toward all one thousand of us waiting outside and grinned. It was Michael Shore.

Sandy gasped. I groaned. Michael! What on earth had he done? Whatever it was, I hoped it wouldn't ruin things for Sandy.

18

Max had the entire story at dinner that night. "Michael and his buddies were smoking in the boys' rest room," Max told us. "Then one of the guys flicked his cigarette onto the toilet seat. It didn't go out—instead it smoldered and made a thick, black smoke. Apparently the smoke appealed to them and—"

"You're kidding!" Nick interrupted. "Didn't the heat set off the overhead sprinklers?"

"The fire wasn't big enough at first," Max went on. "So they lit all the toilet seats on fire and the smoke just poured out of the bathroom. A teacher passed by, panicked, and pulled the fire alarms."

"How'd they know it was Michael Shore?" I asked.

"He was covered in soot," Max said. "His buddies are in trouble, too. But he was the instigator, and the police took him down to the station to make him an example. He will probably be expelled from school. His parents will have to go down to the police station and the school to settle things."

I shook my head. "You mean his mom. Their dad left them—" I cleared my throat because a lump kept rising whenever I thought about my dad. "A long time ago."

Max shrugged. "Well, somebody's got to go down, or he'll be in jail for a long time."

"I'm sure his mother has him out already," Mom said, pouring little dabs of gravy on Stephanie's mashed potatoes. "No mother wants her son to spend the night in jail."

"That may be just what he needs," Uncle Jake interrupted. "It might teach him a lesson."

"I don't know if Michael Shore is the type that learns lessons easily," I said, thinking of the empty liquor bottles in the garbage can. If Michael was drinking even when *everyone* knows how bad it is for you . . .

I shrugged. "This morning he actually looked proud of himself."

"Well, the school will probably expel him, and that will be the end of it," Tom said, summing it up in his lawyer voice. "It's serious, but it's not going to get him a jail sentence or anything. It will probably be left up to his mother to discipline him, and then some other school principal will have to worry about educating Michael Shore."

There wasn't a single Shore in school the next day. Sandy didn't show up for her morning weigh-in, and Sandy, Meredith, and Michael were all on the absentee list. Were they that embarrassed? I tried to understand how Sandy must feel. Sure, it would be embarrassing to have your brother carted away by the police in front of the entire school, but Sandy didn't do anything. Plus, Meredith was Miss Perfect. No one would think less of her for Michael's foul-ups.

But as the day went on and I heard the stories about Michael Shore, I thought I could understand why Meredith and Sandy stayed home. Burning the boys' room was only the latest of Michael's escapades. Last year he jumped from the second-story balcony onto a football player he'd fought the week before. Both of them ended up with broken bones. In middle school he had spray-painted the side of the building with obscene words. "In elementary school," Jaime Stevens told me, "he built a fire under a teacher's car. It's a wonder they found it before the car exploded!"

I knew Michael was a troublemaker, but I never dreamed he was as bad as everyone made him sound. Maybe he was the reason Sandy's family was so weird. Maybe Sandy's dad couldn't cope with having a juvenile delinquent for a son, so he just left. Or maybe Meredith worked so hard to be perfect because she knew Michael was ruining the family name. Maybe Sandy was so shy and awkward because she simply couldn't cope with having a crazy big brother.

How could anyone live with someone like Michael Shore?

19

I tried to be nice to Tom because of my promise to
Nick. Mom noticed it, I guess, and in her own way,
she let me know she appreciated it by patting me on
the back and playfully pulling my hair every now
and then. But when I asked Mom and Tom if they'd
like to chaperon the Spring Fling, Tom lit up like I'd
asked him to give me away at my wedding or something. I thought he'd be pleased, but it irked me that
he was so flattered. Good grief, most parents would
hate chaperon duty. Mom and Tom acted like I'd
given them an academy award.

"Sure, honey, we'd love to be chaperons," Mom
said, after giving Tom a look that said: "I told you
she'd come around."

"There's nothing I'd like better," Tom added, grinning. "I like parties. And since Nick's taking your
friend, I guess we can let Max baby-sit Stephanie,
can't we?"

"Unless he wants to go," Mom said, but Max stuck
his head into the library and cut her off.

"No way," he said simply. "I'll stay here. Adolescent social functions aren't my forte just now."

"We'll be there with bells on," Tom said. He smiled at me. "Thanks for asking."

Gag. I went upstairs, feeling faintly sick to my stomach. The evening had better be worth it.

Sandy was back at school on Friday, but she didn't want to talk about anything that had to do with Michael. "Is everything OK at home?" I persisted as we met outside the gym. "How's Michael? How's Meredith?"

"Michael's home now," Sandy said, quietly, walking with me into the gym. "Mom wasn't able to go get him out of jail until yesterday."

"Did she talk to the principal? Is Michael expelled?"

Sandy gave me a withering glance, and I knew I was asking too much. "Mom came to the school yesterday," she said, finally. "And Michael's at home. And I wish he'd never been born!"

"I'm sorry, Sandy."

Sandy stomped angrily onto the scales, and I was afraid she'd break them. But the scales showed that she weighed 145 pounds! "Look at that!" I cheered. "You've lost fifteen pounds in seven weeks, kiddo! You're doing great!"

Sandy rolled her eyes. "Michael's had us so messed

up, no one's been able to eat," she muttered. "But OK. Now I've got to go see Miss Boyce. I missed the decorating meeting yesterday—"

"Sandy." I laughed. "Look around you. We decorated yesterday, and we used all your ideas."

We had walked into the gym in semidarkness. Now we stepped out of the office corridor where the scales were kept and into the openness of the gym. Sandy's tissue-paper roses were all in place, and the effect was stunning.

"It's beautiful!" Sandy breathed. "Wow, it's really beautiful, isn't it?"

"Yes." I nodded. "I'm sorry you weren't here to help."

"It's OK." Sandy gathered her books, still looking up and around her. "I'll be here tonight, and that's what counts. Nothing—not Meredith or Michael or Mother—nothing is going to stop me tonight!"

I could hardly wait for the last class of the day to end. When the bell finally rang, I met Sandy at my locker, and we raced to the car where Tom and Max were waiting.

"Hurry home," I urged Tom. "Please, I mean. We've got a lot of work to do before tonight."

"Does primping really take three hours?" Tom teased, starting the car. "Honestly, girls, what do you plan to do?"

163

Max rolled his eyes. "Their nails, their hair, their toes, their clothes—"

"Hush," I said, reaching over the seat to bop him on the shoulder. "What do you know about it? Someday when you're old enough to have a social life, you'll want to know how to impress the girls, and I just might not tell you."

"I've got what it takes to impress the girls," Max said, turning around to grin at us.

"Brains?" Sandy asked.

"No," Max answered. "Brown eyes and a dimple. Girls are a cinch."

We laughed and goofed off all the way home, counting the minutes until seven o'clock. Then the Spring Fling would begin.

"So, who did you vote for?" Sandy asked as I rolled her hair around my brush. Her hair was so thick and glossy it seemed to take forever to blow dry.

"Well, you may not believe me, but I voted for you," I told her. "I think you really deserve it. Who did you vote for?"

Sandy blushed. "You deserve it, Cassie, but I voted for Blakely Russo. She just looks like a sweetheart."

"You could have voted for yourself, you know."

"I don't want to win, Cassie. I just want to be there."

I was glad Sandy was beginning to fit in. I decided to let her in on some school gossip. "Andrea Milford was mad at Eric Brandt today because all the guys are voting for Blakely. She said it wasn't fair because all the guys would vote for Blakely, but all the girls' votes would be split between Christine, Andrea, me, and you."

"I really don't think anyone will vote for me," Sandy said, tilting her head as I pulled on her hair with my brush. "The boys only nominated me as a joke. I know that."

"Well, you never know," I said. "Strange things have happened in the past."

"This is the strangest thing of all." Sandy was looking in the mirror. She had applied her makeup the way I showed her, her hair was falling thick and glossy down to her shoulders, and her new outfit was casual and chic. She was stunning. Not a beanpole by any means, but she was a new and improved Sandra Shore.

"If I look as good as you, I'll be lucky," I said, darting into my bathroom to take a shower. "I'll be out in ten minutes, then we'll go downstairs and wait for Chip. Just think, Sandy, in less than thirty minutes we'll be at the Spring Fling!"

Tom drove us in his big Cadillac. At first I thought Nick was going to ruin things by riding up front with Mom and Tom, but he was nice and insisted on riding in the back with me and Chip and Sandy. It was crowded, but it gave me an excuse to sit on Chip's lap. I didn't complain.

The Spring Fling was just a big party with food and fun. There was good music, so some kids were dancing down at one end of the gym. The front of the gym had tables decorated in pretty pastel table-cloths—Sandy's idea. Nick and Chip went to the concession stand to get us drinks and pizza, so Sandy and I slipped into chairs at a table.

Nearly everyone in our class was there, and many had brought dates or friends from other schools. Sandy waved to Jaime Stevens and Christine Miller, and Miss Boyce made a point of coming over to congratulate Sandy on her idea. No one mentioned Michael or the burning bathroom, so that subject was safely out of the way.

Andrea and Eric Brandt showed up together, but it was obvious that Andrea wasn't talking to Eric. She immediately left him by the punch bowl and went off to the girls' room. Eric fell in with Chip and Nick and soon he was at our table.

"Should we save a seat for Andrea?" I asked Eric.

He shrugged. "You can, but it probably won't do any good. She's mad at me."

I knew why, but I kept my mouth closed. Eric winked at me, then looked at Sandy Shore. For a split second he was confused and I realized he honestly didn't recognize her. Then he did, but when he realized she was with Nick, he just looked away. Asking Nick to take Sandy was a good idea—Nick was older, and a good-looking guy. The fact that he was with Sandy made it impossible for jerks like Eric to say anything.

Nick was on his best behavior, too. He brought Sandy a slice of pizza (I noticed she opted for plain cheese—too much fat in pepperoni), and a Diet Coke. He asked her about school, and because I had clued him in, he complimented her on the decorations. And just when the conversation was beginning to lag, he mentioned that he liked sports cars. That's all it took. It seems Sandy has an uncle who manages a race track, and Sandy knows all about sports cars. That was all they talked about for the next hour.

At eight o'clock, Miss Boyce came around and tapped Sandy and me on the shoulder. "We're going to announce the Spring Fling Sweetheart soon," she said, "so we need you girls and your escorts to go to the center of the gym."

The music stopped, the floor cleared, and we five nominees walked stiffly with our escorts to the center of the gym. Chip was a little uncomfortable, so I kept telling dumb jokes to make him feel better. Blakely Russo was with some guy who looked old enough to be in college, and he acted as if he'd rather be anywhere else than at a sophomore party.

Christine Miller was with Colin Triplet, a nice guy who suited her well. Andrea was with Eric, of course, although she still wasn't talking to him. And Sandra Shore stood proudly and relaxed with Nick Harris, the stepbrother I had once despised.

As we stood in the center of the gym, I scanned the crowd for familiar faces. There seemed to be a sea of people, moving and surging, impatient to get on with the party. I couldn't see Mom or Tom anywhere.

"You selected these nominees, and you have chosen a Sweetheart," Miss Boyce said. "With no further ado, let's crown the Sweetheart of this year's Spring Fling! Blakely Russo!"

I thought I could hear a definite moan from about a hundred girls, but the boys all cheered, and Blakely smiled and stepped forward to receive her crown and a bouquet of daisies. Her escort looked even more bored than ever, if that was possible, and from the corner of my eye I could see that Andrea was seething. She was mad enough to spit.

"Congratulations!" Miss Boyce said, and Blakely simpered and thrust her arm into the air for a triumphant victory wave. Then, without any warning, the crowd parted, and a stringy-haired woman staggered out onto the gym floor—and swung a bucket of pink paint at Blakely!

Everything blurred together after that. I remember the woman screamed, "It shoudda been my girl!" and several men, including Tom, grabbed the woman's arms and carried her off the gym floor and out into the night. Blakely Russo, paint dripping from her hair, wailed and screeched, "Why do you all hate me? I'm not after your boyfriends! I promise I'm not!" Miss Boyce yelled for a custodian, and Chip, standing next to me, kept muttering, "I can't believe it! I can't believe it!"

Within five minutes it was all over. Blakely and her escort left, the custodian cleaned up the mess, and Miss Boyce sat in a chair weakly asking for a couple of extra-strength Tylenol. Someone started up the music again, and the party continued as before. It was almost as though the entire incident had been a weird dream or a crazy episode of a television show.

"Who was that woman?" I asked Chip when we were again at our table, but he just shook his head and said again: "I can't believe it!"

Sandy was strangely silent, and Nick was finding it impossible to get her to talk. Finally he kicked me under the table. "Maybe we should go home," he hinted broadly. "Sandy looks tired."

"OK. If you find Mom and Tom, we'll go," I told him. My plan of showing off the new and improved Sandra Shore had lost its appeal. After that bizarre episode with the crazy woman, everything seemed kind of pointless. No one could think about anything else.

Tom and Mom seemed to understand when we said we wanted to go, and they didn't say anything on the way home. I wanted to ask Tom about the woman—after all, he had been one of the men who took her away from the gym. But he didn't seem to want to talk about it. He didn't even ask me where Sandy lived, he just pulled up in front of her house as if he'd been there a thousand times. Then, strangest of all, Tom got out of the car and opened Sandy's door. He put his arm around her and walked her into the house, talking softly to her the entire time. I felt like I was dreaming. Had I missed something?

Mom turned around and saw my startled expression. "That woman at the gym was Sandy's mother," she said. "She's an alcoholic. She was very drunk, and Tom and another man brought her home and put her to bed. He's in there now talking to the kids."

I wondered if Chip and Nick were as surprised as I was. "An alcoholic?" I whispered. "Sandy's mom is an alcoholic?"

"Yes." Mom turned back around away from me.

"She didn't know Sandy was a nominee until yesterday when she had to go to school to get Michael out of trouble. Then she went on a drinking binge and when Sandy didn't win—well, you saw what happened."

The pink paint. I remembered the can of pink paint on the porch, the paint for the trim that Michael was supposed to use on the house.

I felt very, very stupid. All along I had blamed Sandy's problems on so many things—her shyness, her father, her addiction to television, bossy Meredith, trouble-making Michael. But I'd had no idea what was really going on. I didn't really know *anything* about Sandy Shore.

20

I needed to talk to Max. As soon as we got home and Chip left, I headed straight for his room. Stephanie was in there, playing on a blanket, but for once I ignored her and lit into Max. "Max, did you know that Sandy's mother was an alcoholic?" I demanded. "If you knew, why didn't you tell me?"

"Ah," Max said, snapping his fingers. "I didn't know for sure, but I thought it might be something like that. It's a textbook case, you know."

"A textbook case of what?"

Max reached into his desk and pulled out his file on Sandy's diet program. "I began to be suspicious when you described Sandy's personality and eating habits," he said. "So I started taking notes on her personality as well as her diet. Later, when you described Meredith and Michael, I thought we might be looking at an alcoholic family."

I sat on the edge of his bed. "The family isn't alcoholic, just the mother is."

Max shook his head. "When one person is

alcoholic, the entire family is affected. First, men tend to leave alcoholic wives. For some reason, though, women tend to stay with alcoholic husbands." He looked up and squinted at me. "I guess women are more sympathetic or something."

I shook my head. "I still don't understand."

"Look, it's simple. When someone is an alcoholic, the other family members usually try to deny or hide the problem. The oldest child, in this case Meredith, tries to fulfill the responsibilities of the parent. When you said Meredith was bossy, well, that fits perfectly. She doesn't want anyone to know that her mother isn't doing what she should do, so Meredith works hard to cover it up. She overcompensates."

"So why doesn't Michael overcompensate?"

"Because he's the family scapegoat. He wants attention, even if it's negative. In a strange way, he wants to be blamed for the family's problems."

"That's crazy."

"No, it's not."

"What about Sandy?"

"From what you've told me, I believe Sandy is the lost child in the family. She doesn't want to make waves. She doesn't want to do anything, either positive or negative. She just wants to be left alone."

It was as though Max knew Sandy better than I

did. Why hadn't I been able to see all of this? "I never dreamed Sandy's mother had a problem," I whispered. "But I should have known. Sandy had a habit of lying about her family, and I never even saw her mother."

"I thought something was funny when you said Sandy didn't want you to come over," Max said, closing his folder. "The children of alcoholics are usually ashamed to bring friends home. They never know what their parent might do."

"Mrs. Shore was asleep when I was there."

"She was probably passed out or drunk."

"Why didn't Sandy or Meredith tell someone?"

"They were ashamed." Max picked Stephanie up off the blanket, and he looked strange, like a wise old man in a ten-year-old body. "That's why Michael didn't want you to see the empty bottles in the trash. Michael, Sandy, and Meredith all probably think it's somehow their fault their mother drinks. Especially after Michael got into trouble at school—all three kids were ashamed to show their faces. Children of alcoholics also believe they can't trust anybody but themselves . . . so they had to stick together."

The pieces were beginning to fit together. No wonder Sandy resisted my friendship at first! No wonder she didn't want to change. Going on a diet for her must have seemed impossible, because if her mother couldn't stay away from alcohol, how could Sandy learn to stay away from food?

But she had done it. She had learned to eat right, she had made new friends, and she had come a long way out of her shell. After tonight, though, could she survive the shame she must be feeling?

"What happens now?" I asked Max. "Sandy's mother came to the Spring Fling tonight and threw paint on Blakely Russo."

Max whistled. "You're kidding."

"No. Tom and some other man took her home, so they know the whole story. Tom will probably tell Miss Boyce, too."

"They all need help. But Miss Boyce should know about Alateen, so the Shore kids can get help if they want to."

"What's Alateen?"

"It's an organization for teenagers who have alcoholic parents. It's sort of a companion organization of Alcoholics Anonymous. That's what Mrs. Shore needs . . . but even if she doesn't get help, the kids can. There are lots of church counselors who would be willing to help. All Sandy has to do is ask."

"I'll make sure she does. I know my youth pastor would talk to her."

There was a knock on the door, and Mom and

Tom came into the room. "Cassie, we were proud of the way you handled yourself tonight," Mom said, taking the baby from Max. "It must have been horrible to see your friend's mother in that condition."

"I didn't know," I said simply. "I didn't know anything about it. I had tried to help Sandy lose weight so you wouldn't think I was self-centered, but I had no idea what she really needed." I felt tears stinging at my eyes.

Mom sat down on the bed next to me and lowered Stephanie back down to the floor. "It's OK, honey. We saw how hard you were working with Sandy. You didn't have to prove anything to us. You're a good kid, but you're a normal kid. I don't think you're any more self-centered than anyone else."

"We all goof up sometimes," Tom said, sitting in the empty space on my other side. "But we're a family, and we've got to stick together."

I suddenly realized how lucky I was. I had a great mom, two uniquely weird brothers, a darling baby sister . . . and Tom. Tom had been a hero tonight, and I was glad to admit it. But I also had a dad. . . .

"I love my dad," I blurted out.

Tom's head jerked back, but he was quick to respond: "I know you do."

"But I like you, too."

I didn't want him to gush or anything, and thankfully, he didn't. Tom just patted me on the shoulder and said, "I know that, too."

"Come on, it's been a long night and I'm tired," Mom said, pulling me up. "Tomorrow morning Tom is going to the Shores' house to see how we can help them. You can go too, Cass, if you want to see Sandy."

Tom and I. Together. We'd go help Sandy Shore the much adored. I had tried to help her alone, thinking I would do it for God, but he knew Sandy needed more than a make-over.

"OK. I'd like that," I said. "But right now I'm ready for bed. I'm so tired I could sleep for a week."

"Did you know that Al Herpin never slept in his ninety-four years of life?" Max asked. "He lived in Trenton, New Jersey, and he never even owned a bed. People used to stay up and try to catch him sleeping, but he never slept. He—"

"Good night, Max!" Mom, Tom, and I yelled together.

If you or someone you love is struggling with substance abuse or an eating disorder, consider calling one of the following agencies:

Substance Abusers Victorious
P. O. Box 699
Dayton, Tennessee 37321-0699
Substance Abusers Victorious is a Christian organization dedicated to helping substance abusers find victory over their addictions through new life in Christ.

RAPHA
800-227-2657
Through hospital facilities, RAPHA offers help for kids and adults who are struggling with substance abuse. RAPHA's program involves Christ-centered counseling and therapy.

The National Federation of Parents for Drug-Free
  Youth
800-554-KIDS
Call between 9:00 A.M. and 5:00 P.M. EST for information and referrals.

800-662-HELP
This confidential information and referral line directs callers to cocaine abuse treatment centers and offers free materials on drug abuse.

Cocaine Helpline
800-COCAINE
Cocaine Helpline offers round-the-clock information and referral service. Reformed cocaine addicts offer guidance and refer drug users and parents to treatment centers and family learning centers.

Alcoholics Anonymous
800-344-2666
Al-Anon offers information about Alateen chapters throughout the United States. The meetings are free, and they ask no questions.

ANAD: The National Association of Anorexia
  Nervosa and Associated Disorders
(Illinois) 708-831-3438

American Anorexia/Bulemia Association, Inc.
(New York) 212-734-1114